LOUIZA MAY ARNOLD

THE CRIMSON OBSESSION

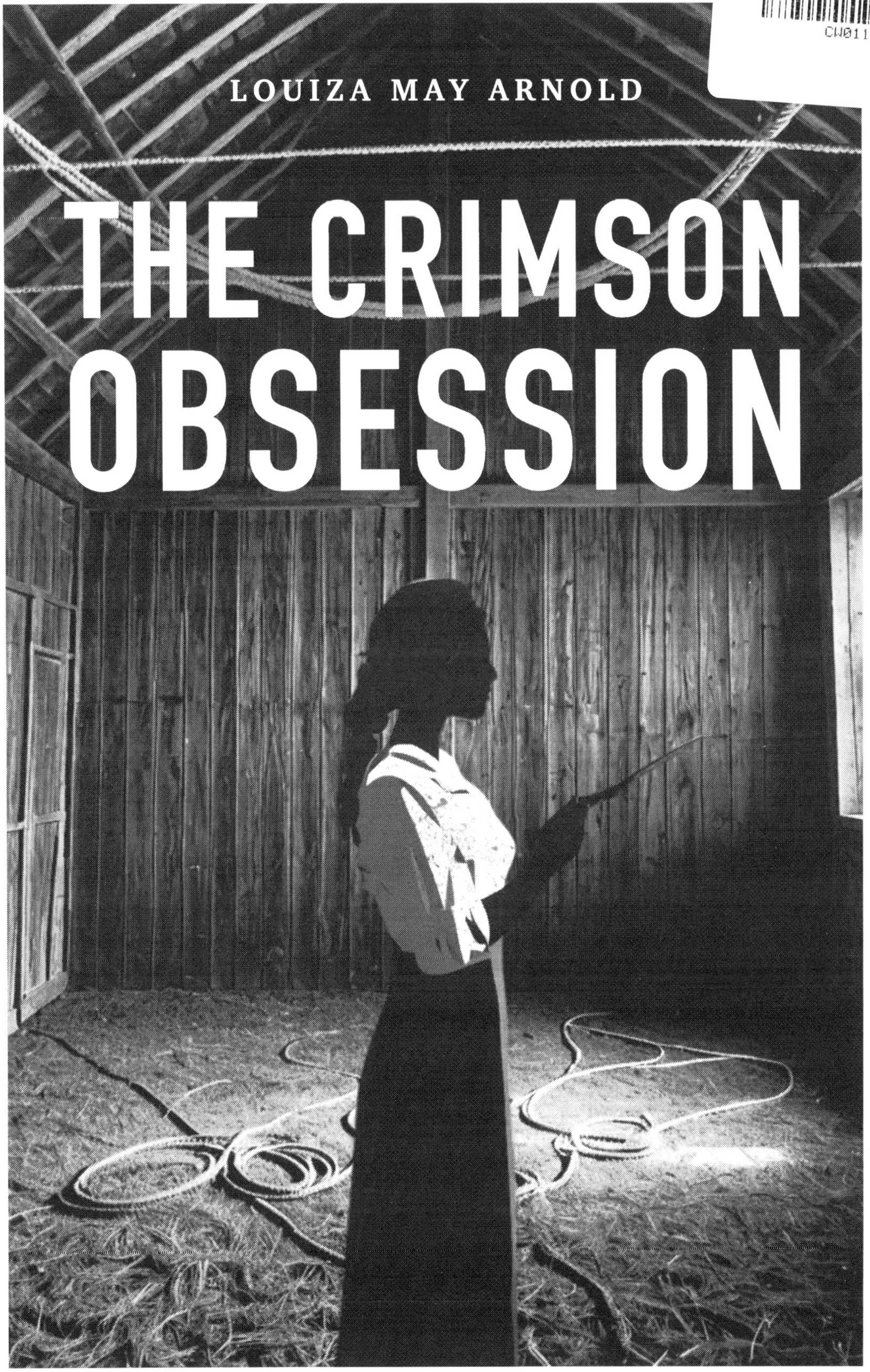

The Thrill Of The Chase

ONE

In the quiet town of Bridgefield, where the sun dipped below the horizon with a deceptive calm, a shadow lurked among the ordinary. The streets, lined with picket fences and blooming gardens, were oblivious to the chilling reality that a murderer walked among them. Unlike the cliche descriptions of tormented souls or those battling inner demons, this killer thrived in a realm devoid of mental health struggles. There were no whispers of trauma or haunting memories—just a chillingly composed individual, driven by a cold and calculated desire. As the first drops of rain began to fall, the tranquility of Bridgefield would soon be shattered, and the darkness that resided within, one of their own would unveil itself in the most terrifying of ways. That individual is me.

You're probably wondering how I manage to carve out the time to pen this little memoir of mine. After all, every killer has their collection of trinkets, don't they? Some might keep trophies from their victims, but my prized possession is this—writing it all down. It's a bit of a gamble, I admit. The thought of someone stumbling upon this cheerful little novel and turning me in does send an electrifying jolt through my veins. Yet, honestly? I couldn't care less. In fact, I find myself almost craving the moment when I get caught. There's a thrill in the chase, a delicious tension that's hard to resist, and I'm more than ready to embrace whatever consequences lie ahead.

But not just yet. There's one more person I have my sights set on—a final act to complete before I let the world in on my little secret. I've been watching her for a while now, noting her routine as she walks to and from work, blissfully unaware of the shadow that lingers just out of sight. The anticipation builds with each passing day, and I can almost taste the excitement that comes with the thought of her being my next conquest. Just one more, and then I'll be ready for whatever comes next,

Killing has become my drug, an intoxicating high that courses through my veins, igniting every nerve ending with a thrill that nothing else can replicate. The moment I take a life, the world around me blurs into insignificance, and all that remains is the pulsating rush of adrenaline. It's a sensation far more potent than any substance I could imagine, a euphoric escape from the mundane reality of everyday existence.

Each act is a carefully orchestrated symphony, a dance between life and death, and I am both the conductor and the audience. The anticipation builds like a finely tuned crescendo, and when the moment finally arrives, it's as if time stands still. The exhilaration is overwhelming, a sweet release that envelops me in a haze of bliss. I find myself craving that rush, counting down the days between each encounter like a junkie waiting for their next fix.

With every kill, I become more deeply entrenched in this dark addiction. The thrill of the hunt, the meticulous planning, the final moment—it's a cycle I can't seem to escape. And remember, though, I'm not a psychopath; I have no diagnosed mental health issues. I simply love to kill. It's not just about the act itself; it's about the power I wield, the control I exert over life and death. As I sink deeper into this abyss, I know that I'll never truly be satisfied until I take another life, feeding this insatiable craving that has become my very existence.

Adrenaline surges through my body like a tidal wave, igniting every nerve ending and sharpening my senses to a razor's edge. In those moments, everything around me blurs into insignificance, and all that matters is the thrill coursing through my veins. This hormone, also known as epinephrine, heightens my awareness and allows me to focus intently on the task at hand, as if the world has slowed down just for me.

There's a peculiar euphoria that accompanies this rush, a feeling of invincibility that makes me feel more alive than ever. The surge of adrenaline stimulates the release of glucose and fatty acids into my bloodstream, providing me with a quick energy boost that is vital in high-pressure situations. I have no pains or trauma, I just love to get high on adrenaline. Oh, I am aware that this rush can't last indefinitely. Prolonged exposure to elevated levels of adrenaline, often due to chronic stress, can lead to negative health consequences, including anxiety disorders and cardiovascular problems. Look at me being clever hey! Yet, in those fleeting moments, I'm consumed by the thrill, unable to resist the compelling urge to chase that feeling again and again, revelling in the terrific carnage it brings.

I've always been different, but not in the way most people think. My childhood was filled with the same mundane routines as anyone else's—school, family dinners, and weekend outings. I grew up in a stable home, with my mother as a stay-at-home mum, tirelessly looking after me and my older brother. She was the kind of woman who faded into the background, her presence hardly noticed. With her drab clothing and a face that time had not been kind to, she embodied a kind of boring normalcy that both repelled and intrigued me.

My father, on the other hand, was a whirlwind of energy. A hard-working businessman, he was the one who kept our family afloat. His sense of humour was infectious; he could light up a room with his laughter and turn the mundane into something extraordinary. I always looked forward to the sound of his voice after a long day, sharing stories and jokes that made even the dullest family dinner feel vibrant. My father was my anchor, a stark contrast to my mother's dull presence, and I often found myself caught between their two worlds.

Then there was my older brother, who was odd and wonderfully weird in his own right. Diagnosed with autism, he often preferred the solitude of his room, retreating into worlds of his own creation. I admired his brilliance, the way he could lose himself in complex puzzles or elaborate video games, but I also felt a distance between us. While I craved connection and excitement, he seemed content in his isolation, and I often found myself wondering what went on in that mind of his.

While my peers found joy in sports, friendships, and hobbies, I felt a persistent emptiness inside me that I couldn't quite articulate. They laughed and connected over shared experiences, while I stood at the edge, observing but never fully engaging. I often found solace in the pages of books and the flickering glow of the television, losing myself in stories of adventure and excitement, longing for a thrill that remained just out of reach.

But it was the murder documentaries that truly captivated me. As a child, I would sit wide-eyed in front of the screen, absorbing every detail of the twisted tales of obsession and chaos. I was fascinated by the psychology behind these heinous acts, drawn to the dark allure that came with each chilling narrative. It was more than just entertainment; it was an awakening. These stories fed a hunger within me, a thirst for understanding the depths of human nature and the shadows lurking within.

I've always been a slim girl, not anorexic but fit and healthy, with shoulder-length blonde hair that catches the light just right, framing my face in a way that often draws attention. My green eyes, vibrant and full of life, can be disarming, almost inviting. But there's a depth there that few have ever glimpsed. The truth is, beneath that exterior lies a spirit that craves more than what the world has to offer.

As I grew older, I began to explore what made me feel truly alive, seeking thrills that could stir something deep within. It started with small acts of rebellion—breaking rules, pushing boundaries—but nothing ever quite satisfied that insatiable hunger for excitement. I found myself drawn to the thrill of danger, the rush that comes with stepping outside the lines of normalcy.

Then, one fateful day, I stumbled upon the exhilarating rush of adrenaline. It was intoxicating, a drug that ignited every fibre of my being. With each heartbeat, I felt more alive, more powerful. It was as if I had discovered a hidden part of myself, one that craved not just excitement, but the ultimate expression of control: taking a life.

I remember the first time I crossed that line. The anticipation built within me, a palpable energy that thrummed in my veins. It was exhilarating, a symphony of emotions that swirled within me—fear, exhilaration, and an overwhelming sense of power. I didn't feel guilty or remorseful; instead, I felt liberated. The act itself became a ritual, a way to escape the suffocating normalcy of life.

But there was something specific about my choice of victims that seemed to deepen my connection to the thrill: I only killed women. There was a magnetic pull, an inexplicable desire that drove me to seek out those who shared my own essence. Perhaps it was the beauty in their vulnerability, or the thrill of overpowering someone who looked like me. Whatever the reason, each woman I targeted became a reflection of my unfulfilled desires, each act a twisted expression of control and liberation.

As I delved deeper into this obsession, I found myself drawn to the thrill of the hunt. Every encounter became an elaborate game; each victim a pawn in my twisted pursuit of ecstasy. I thrived on the planning, the anticipation, and the final moment when everything came together in a rush of adrenaline that left me breathless.

I remember one particular night, the city lights twinkling like stars against the dark sky, as I stalked my next target. The air was electric, charged with potential. My heart raced in time with the rhythm of my footsteps. The thrill of the chase was intoxicating, and I could feel the weight of my desires pressing against my chest. It was in that moment, under the cloak of darkness, that I truly felt alive.

I'm not a monster; I'm simply someone who has embraced my desires fully. I don't carry the weight of trauma or a troubled past, nor do I grapple with mental health issues. I've found my purpose in the chaos, and with each life I take, I feel more alive than ever. The world may never understand, but I've come to accept that I'm driven by an unquenchable thirst for the thrill that only I can experience. I am a woman who loves other women, finding beauty and connection in the unexpected, yet my heart also craves the wildness of life in all its forms. Each heartbeat reminds me that I'm alive, and I'll do whatever it takes to keep that feeling burning bright.

Jessica

TWO

....

I was fifteen when my life took a turn I never expected, all because of Jessica. She was like a mirror image of me—slim, blonde, with green eyes that sparkled with mischief and an adventurous spirit. From the moment we met, an unexplainable connection sparked between us. We were inseparable, bonding over our shared interests and the thrill of defying the mundane. Jessica was the reason I discovered my attraction to women; she awakened something within me that I didn't even know existed.

With her, every moment felt electric. Our laughter echoed through the hallways of our school, and late-night secrets turned into whispered confessions that drew us closer. We often found ourselves lost in each other's eyes, sharing dreams and fears, our souls intertwining in a way that felt profound. It was intoxicating, the way she made me feel alive. Jessica was everything I had been searching for, a kindred spirit who matched my energy and passion.

As our relationship blossomed, I found myself captivated by her every move. The way she tossed her hair over her shoulder or how her laughter could light up even the dullest of days. We explored the world around us, diving headfirst into adventures that felt limitless. I remember the first time we held hands, a simple gesture that sent shivers down my spine. Every touch ignited a fire that coursed through my veins, awakening desires I hadn't yet acknowledged.

But as time went on, I felt an insatiable hunger growing within me, one that extended beyond the boundaries of our relationship. The thrill of being with Jessica was exhilarating, but there was a darkness lurking beneath the surface, a desire for control that began to intertwine with my feelings for her. I couldn't help but wonder what it would feel like to take that connection to an entirely different level.

Those thoughts soon turned into an obsession. I became fixated on the idea of Jessica, my first love and first victim. She epitomised everything I cherished, yet I found myself wanting more. The intensity of our bond transformed into a dangerous game that I felt compelled to play. The line between love and desire blurred, and I was caught in a whirlwind of emotion that both thrilled and terrified me.

The day I crossed that line is etched into my memory forever. It was a moment of liberation, a release of all the pent-up energy that had been building within me. I didn't feel guilty or remorseful; instead, I felt empowered. In a way, I was reclaiming a part of myself that had been longing for expression, and Jessica, so much like me, became the perfect reflection of that dark urge.

With her, the thrill of the hunt transformed into an exhilarating game, and I was both the player and the prize. Each heartbeat reminded me that I was alive, and in that moment, I embraced the chaos that accompanied my desires. Jessica was no longer just my first love; she had become the embodiment of everything I craved, and I was determined to take that connection to the ultimate extreme.

I remember the first night I spent at Jessica's house like it was yesterday—an evening that promised adventure, mischief, and an absurd amount of popcorn. Her parents were out for the night, leaving us with the whole house to ourselves—a perfect setup for what would become a legendary night. As I stepped through the door, the smell of buttery popcorn hit me like a warm hug, mingling with the faint aroma of what I could only assume was her mom's questionable cooking experiments.

"Welcome to my lair!" she declared dramatically, throwing her arms open as if she were unveiling a grand palace. I couldn't help but laugh. It felt like the start of a horror movie, but instead of a creepy basement, we had a perfectly normal living room full of snacks.

"Did you prepare for this night with a full snack arsenal?" I asked, eyeing the mountain of goodies piled high on the coffee table. There were gummy bears, chips, and enough chocolate to fuel a small country.

"Of course! What's a horror movie night without enough sugar to send us into a sugar-induced panic?" she grinned, her eyes gleaming with mischief. "Now, let's get this party started! We're kicking it off with Saw! You ready to be traumatised?"

I raised an eyebrow. "You really know how to set the mood, don't you?" But honestly, I was excited. The combination of horror films and Jessica was a heady mix that made my heart race for all the right reasons.

As the movie started, I glanced at her, and there she was—completely enthralled. While I squirmed at the graphic scenes, she practically sparkled with delight. "This is like watching a twisted art exhibit!" she exclaimed, her eyes wide. "Look at the creativity! I mean, who even thinks of these traps?"

"Seriously, I'd be like, 'Hey, Jigsaw, let's just grab some ice cream and talk about our feelings instead of this whole 'traps and torture' thing,'" I joked.

She burst into laughter, clutching her stomach. "Exactly! But I'd probably end up as the main course if I tried to negotiate!"

As the movie progressed, I found myself torn between the bizarre gore and the enchanting girl beside me. Jessica was a delightful mix of charmingly odd and hilariously dark. It was intoxicating, and I couldn't help but admire how she embraced her quirks. Her life hadn't been easy, coming from a broken home, but she carried her baggage like a badge of honour, and I admired her for it.

When the credits finally rolled, Jessica turned to me, her face lit up with a devilish grin. "So, ready for the sequel? I promise it's even more twisted!"

"Hold on there, horror queen! I think I need a breather after that," I said, trying to regain my composure.

"How about we watch something less… terrifying? Like a rom-com?"

"Boring!" she declared, dramatically rolling her eyes.

But as the night wore on, the atmosphere shifted. The thrill of the horror films hung in the air like a tantalising aftertaste, and our playful banter started to fade. We were inching closer together on the couch, and suddenly, the world outside her living room ceased to exist.

Before I knew it, we were kissing, and let me tell you, it was like stepping into a wild dream. Jessica's hands tangled in my hair, pulling me closer, and I felt this rush of exhilaration that made my stomach flip. It was thrilling, tender, and filled with an unspoken promise.

Somewhere between the popcorn and the horror, the night took a decidedly unexpected turn. "You know," she whispered, her voice teasingly low, "I kind of like it when things get a little rough."

I raised an eyebrow, intrigued. "Rough? Like Saw level rough? Because I'm not sure I'm ready to saw off any limbs tonight!"

She chuckled, biting her lip in a way that made my heart race. "Not quite that extreme, but let's just say I enjoy a bit of biting."

"Biting? Like, 'I'm gonna take a chunk out of you' kind of biting?" I asked, half-laughing, half-curious.

"Exactly! It's like a love bite, but with a side of 'please don't call the cops!'" she replied, her eyes sparkling with mischief.

"Well, in that case…" I leaned in closer, testing the waters as I playfully nipped at her neck. "Like this?"

"Perfect!" she breathed, her eyes lighting up with delight.

And just like that, the horror movie night transformed into something much more thrilling. The boundaries between love and desire blurred, and I found myself diving headfirst into this wild exploration with Jessica. It was a mix of laughter, unexpected twists, and a little bit of biting—just enough to keep things interesting.

As the credits rolled on the final film, the atmosphere was thick with a heady mix of fear and exhilaration. I turned to Jessica, her eyes wide and sparkling like they were about to pop out of her head. We were sprawled across the bed, the remnants of popcorn scattered around us like the aftermath of a snack explosion. "That last movie was ridiculous!" I exclaimed, laughter bubbling up. "I mean, who even thinks of running upstairs when the creepy killer is downstairs? Talk about poor decision-making!"

Jessica giggled, her laughter infectious. "Right? It's like, 'Sure, let's go to the attic where the axe murderer is probably waiting with a cup of tea!'" She rolled her eyes dramatically, and I couldn't help but chuckle along with her.

"Your name is beautiful, Dahlia," she said, her voice softening as she brushed a stray hair from my face. "It reminds me of flowers—dark, mysterious, and alluring. Just like you."

I smirked, leaning closer. "Beautiful, huh? Well, you know what they say about flowers: they can be enchanting, but they can also have thorns."

"True," she replied, her eyes glinting mischievously. "But I like a little danger. It makes life exciting!"

"Exciting, indeed!" I said, raising an eyebrow. "But let's not go overboard; I don't want to end up on a true crime documentary."

As we lay there, the warmth of her body against mine was intoxicating, but so was the thrill of what we'd just watched. "What if we could create our own horror movie experience? A little adventure that makes our hearts race even faster than those ridiculous films?"

"Are we talking about a horror-themed escape room or, like, kidnapping someone?" she asked, half-laughing, half-serious.

"Why not both?" I grinned, my heart racing at the thought. "We could lure someone in, like a couple of devious little pixies. We'd be the ultimate horror duo! Imagine the epic plot twist when we reveal that we're just here to give them a scare—and potentially steal their snacks!"

Jessica burst into laughter, clutching her stomach. "You mean to tell me that our grand plan is to frighten someone just to get their popcorn? That's the real horror here!"

"Exactly! It's the perfect plan—no one ever suspects the cute girls with a penchant for popcorn theft. We just need to find our unsuspecting victim."

"Maybe we should hang up a sign: 'Adventurous souls needed for a thrilling experience. Snacks provided!'" she suggested, her eyes sparkling with mischief.

"Perfect!" I exclaimed. "And when they show up, we can put on our best horror movie faces, maybe even some fake blood. We could be like, 'Welcome to your worst nightmare! But first, let's have a snack break!'"

At that moment, I could see the wheels turning in her head, the thrill of the idea pulling her in. "I love it! But what if they're actually scary? What if they have a pet snake or something?"

"Then we just have to be sneakier than the snake!" I laughed, my mind racing with the possibilities. "We could practice our best horror movie screams just in case. Or we could dress up as the characters we love to mock—be the ultimate horror parody team!"

Jessica's laughter rang out again, bright and infectious. "I can already see it. 'Watch out! It's the terrifying Dahlia, the flower with a penchant for popcorn and mayhem!'"

"Exactly! And I'll be all like, 'Fear me, I come from a long line of bloodthirsty daisies!'" I exclaimed, throwing my hands up dramatically.

As we giggled in our little cocoon of chaos, the lines between thrill and humour began to blur. "Let's make tonight unforgettable," I whispered, my voice low and playful. "Just imagine the stories we could tell."

"Or the horror movie we could accidentally create!" she replied, her eyes dancing with excitement.

"Adventure awaits, my daring accomplice!" I declared, pretending to wield an imaginary sword. "Now, shall we plot our popcorn heist?"

As Jessica nodded, her laughter echoing in the room, I realised how far we were willing to go for a little thrill—and maybe a lot of popcorn. The shadows of the night began to call to us, and who knew? Maybe this was just the beginning of our delightfully twisted escapade.

Months slid by like a well-oiled horror movie montage, each night with Jessica transforming into a whirlwind of laughter, mischief, and thrilling escapades. We became experts in the art of 'snack theft and scare tactics,' crafting elaborate plots that would make even the most seasoned horror directors nod in approval—or confusion. We'd dress up as gory versions of our favourite characters, complete with ridiculous props we'd cobbled together from the depths of our closets. Who knew that a feather boa could look so terrifying when paired with a plastic axe?

Our adventures grew bolder, and with every new escapade, our bond deepened. One evening, while we were attempting to recreate a horror film scene in my backyard (which mostly involved us shrieking and tripping over garden gnomes), Jessica turned to me with a glint in her eye that hinted at something more. "I've got a surprise for you," she announced, her voice dripping with intrigue.

A few weeks later, as my sixteenth birthday rolled around, Jessica presented me with a gift that was both thrilling and utterly hilarious. Wrapped in shiny black paper with a big red bow that looked suspiciously like it had been pilfered from a Christmas present, I unwrapped it to find… a knife.

But not just any knife. This was a knife that could only be described as a gleaming piece of art, albeit one crafted for a horror movie set. The blade was long and slender, gleaming like it had been polished by the very gods of mischief themselves! It caught the light in a way that was almost dramatic—like it was auditioning for a starring role in a slasher flick. "Behold!" Jessica exclaimed, her arms wide as if presenting the Holy Grail. "Your very own 'Dahlia's Delight' knife!"

"What am I supposed to do with this?" I laughed, holding it up. "Cut cake? Or maybe slice through the very fabric of reality?"

"Both, obviously!" she grinned, her eyes sparkling with that familiar mischief. "But mostly cake. And also, you know, for when we need to fend off any unsuspecting snack-stealers!"

The handle was a marvel in itself—a deep crimson, like it had been crafted from the heart of a particularly dramatic flower, and shaped to fit snugly in my palm. It had little grooves that made it feel almost like it was meant to dance between my fingers, begging to be brandished in a wildly exaggerated fashion, perhaps with a flourish or two that would make any horror villain proud.

"Do you see those little details?" Jessica pointed out. "Those are not just for show; they're designed for maximum grip! You could practically carve a pumpkin while fending off a creepy clown!"

I couldn't help but snicker at that thought. "Right! Because nothing says 'happy birthday' like a horror-themed pumpkin carving while being chased by a clown!"

"Exactly! And just think of all the potential! We could even start a new trend—'Knife Skills for the Horror Enthusiast!'" she declared, her eyes wide with creativity. "We'll be the talk of the town!"

With the knife in hand, our nights became even more experimental. We'd concoct elaborate horror-themed dinners where we'd pretend we were chefs in a twisted cooking show, using the knife to slice through imaginary tension as we cackled over our "disgusting but gourmet" concoctions. We'd take turns playing the role of the unsuspecting victim, while the other wielded the knife dramatically, our laughter echoing into the night as we playfully screamed and flailed, trying to outdo each other with the most ridiculous horror tropes.

"Look out! It's the deadly Dahlia, armed and ready to serve her guests… a lovely slice of cake!" I'd yell, brandishing the knife like a sword, while Jessica laughed so hard she nearly fell off her chair.

We transformed the mundane into the extraordinary, each night filled with experiments that blurred the lines between horror and hilarity. My sixteenth birthday had gifted me more than just a knife; it had opened the door to a fantastical world where we could laugh in the face of fear, dance with danger, and carve out our own unique brand of thrilling chaos. With Jessica by my side, I knew we were just getting started on this delightfully twisted journey together.

One evening, as we lounged in my dimly lit room surrounded by the remnants of our latest snack heist, I couldn't shake the playful idea that had been brewing in my head all day. The knife, with its gleaming blade and wickedly beautiful handle, had become a symbol of all our thrilling adventures together. I turned to Jessica, who was flicking popcorn kernels at me and giggling, her laughter brightening the room.

"Hey, Jess," I said, suddenly feeling a rush of mischief. "What do you think about using the knife in a more… intimate setting?"

Her eyes widened, a mix of surprise and amusement dancing across her features. "You mean like a candlelit dinner? Or are we talking about something much more scandalous?"

I grinned, loving where this was heading. "Oh, I was thinking more along the lines of a candlelit bedroom experience. You know, a bit of dramatic flair."

She raised an eyebrow, a smirk creeping onto her lips. "You're suggesting we turn your room into a horror-themed boudoir, complete with flickering candles and a knife? I love it!"

With that, we set to work creating our little candlelit sanctuary. I rummaged through my drawer, pulling out the mismatched candles I'd collected over the years—some barely used, others slightly melted from previous attempts at mood-setting. We arranged them around the room, the soft glow casting flickering shadows on the walls and making everything feel just a tad more mysterious.

"Right, now for the pièce de résistance!" I announced dramatically, holding up the knife. Its blade reflected the candlelight, creating a glimmering effect that made it look almost magical.

Jessica bit her lip, her excitement palpable as she settled onto the bed. "Okay, but you have to promise me one thing," she said, her voice teasing. "No accidental 'oops' moments, alright? I'd rather not become a horror story myself!"

"Cross my heart!" I said, holding the knife with exaggerated seriousness, as if it were the most delicate object in the world. "Now, let's create our own little plot twist."

With the atmosphere thick with anticipation, I took a moment to admire the way the candlelight danced across Jessica's face, illuminating her features in a soft glow. She looked both stunning and slightly mischievous, and I felt a thrill course through me.

I moved closer, the knife held lightly in my hand, and traced its cool blade along her arm, just barely touching her skin. "I can't believe we're doing this," I murmured, my heart racing with a mix of excitement and the thrill of the unknown.

Jessica shivered, her breath hitching slightly. "This is definitely not what I expected for tonight!"

"Just think of it as a little exploration," I said, the knife gliding down her arm, tracing delicate patterns that sent shivers of exhilaration through us both. "A little thrill, a little danger... and a whole lot of fun."

As I continued to trace the knife across her skin, I felt an exhilarating rush. The contrast of the cold metal against her warmth was electrifying, and I could see her eyes widen with the thrill of it all. There was something delightfully twisted about the entire scene—two girls playing with danger in the most intimate way possible, wrapped in candlelight and laughter.

"Just remember," she said with a cheeky grin, "if you cut me, you're responsible for everything! Tell my family I loved them dearly!'

"Don't worry," I laughed, "I'll will but I'll charge them for all the snacks you've made me buy instead!"

The room filled with our laughter, the knife becoming a playful extension of our shared humour, turning what could have been a tense moment into a delightful adventure. With each careful movement, we danced on the edge of thrill and laughter, creating our own version of a twisted fairy tale—one where the danger was just a flick of the wrist away, but the fun was always at the forefront, until it wasn't.

As the months rolled on, the whirlwind of laughter and mischief that had defined my time with Jessica began to fade. With the start of college, she was swept up into a new world filled with fresh faces and new experiences. I watched from the sidelines, my heart twisting with a pang of jealousy that I couldn't quite shake off.

It was strange to see her with her new friends—an eclectic group that seemed to thrive on the very things we used to enjoy. They'd go on day trips, exploring the city and posting pictures of their laughter and adventures on social media. Each notification that lit up my phone felt like a dagger, twisting deeper into my chest. While they frolicked in the sun, I was tucked away in my own world, buried in the rigours of my apprenticeship in the medical sector.

I had chosen this path, and part of me felt proud to be taking the leap into something serious, but another part of me couldn't help but feel abandoned. Our horror movie nights had turned into lonely evenings spent staring at walls, the thrill of our relationship replaced with a painful emptiness.

When I did see Jessica, she was brimming with energy, her stories filled with laughter and excitement. "You should come to the library with me sometime!" she suggested one evening, her eyes alight with enthusiasm. "It'll be fun! We can study together!"

But I could only manage a tight smile, my stomach churning at the thought of being part of her new life. "Yeah, maybe," I said, my voice lacking the enthusiasm I wished I could muster. The truth was, I didn't want to be a part of that world—filled with her new friends and their laughter that felt like an echo of what we once had.

As the weeks passed, the jealousy festered within me like a dark cloud. I found myself scrolling through her social media, obsessively analysing every photo, every caption. I'd watch her smile, that beautiful smile that had once been reserved for our late-night escapades, now shared with people I barely knew. They looked so happy, and I couldn't help but feel like a ghost—haunting the periphery of her life, desperately trying to cling onto the remnants of what we had shared.

One evening, after another day spent labouring over medical textbooks, I found myself alone in my room, the weight of my thoughts suffocating. I picked up the knife Jessica had gifted me, its blade glinting ominously in the dim light. It had once symbolised our playful adventures, but now it felt like a reminder of everything I was losing.

What had started as a thrilling journey was morphing into something darker. I was spiralling, caught between the shadows of my jealousy and the longing for the connection we onceAs the months slipped by, I noticed a gradual shift in Jessica's behaviour. The horror movie marathons and our thrilling knife play sessions became fewer and farther between. Instead, she would often choose to spend her time studying at the library or going on outings with a new group of friends she had made since starting college.

The change didn't sit well with me. A growing sense of jealousy began to fester, like a dark cloud slowly obscuring the vibrant world we had once shared. I couldn't help but feel replaced, pushed aside in favour of these new people who had somehow managed to steal Jessica's attention away from me.

Gone were the nights where we would giggle and plan our next delightfully twisted adventure. Now, Jessica would make excuses, claiming she needed to focus on her studies or that her new friends had organised some mundane outing that she couldn't miss. I would watch helplessly as she slipped away, my heart sinking with each departure.

In a bid to distract myself from the gnawing loneliness, I had chosen to forgo college and instead pursue an apprenticeship in the medical sector. The work was demanding, but it provided a welcome distraction from the void Jessica's absence had left. I threw myself into my studies, immersing myself in the intricacies of anatomy and the delicate art of surgical procedures.

Yet, no matter how engrossed I became in my work, Jessica's absence continued to weigh heavily on my mind. I found myself constantly checking my phone, hoping for a message, a call, anything that would rekindle the connection we had once shared. But the messages grew fewer, the calls more sporadic, and the distance between us felt like an ever-widening chasm.

The knife, once a symbol of our shared thrill and mischief, now lay forgotten in my drawer, a silent reminder of the life we had once lived. The thought of it sent a pang of sorrow through me, a longing for the days when our laughter had filled the air and the world had seemed so full of possibility.

As the months passed, my jealousy began to morph into something darker, a smouldering resentment that threatened to consume me. I watched bitterly as Jessica's new friends swept her away, their laughter and camaraderie a stark contrast to the emptiness I felt. It was as if they had stolen a part of her, a part that had once been mine.

The once-vibrant and mischievous Dahlia was slowly being replaced by a colder, more withdrawn version of myself. The thrill had been replaced by a dull ache, and the laughter had been silenced by the weight of my growing bitterness.

I knew I needed to do something, to find a way to reclaim the connection we had once shared. But the more I tried to reach out, the more Jessica seemed to pull away, her attention focused on this new life she had built without me. The thought of losing her entirely was a terrifying prospect, one that I was unwilling to entertain.

As I lay awake at night, the knife glinting in the moonlight, I began to formulate a plan – a way to bring Jessica back to me, to reignite the spark that had once burned so brightly between us. The path ahead at the time was uncertain, but I knew I was determined to do whatever it took to reclaim what was rightfully mine, forever.

When the weekend finally arrived, I spent the morning preparing for Jessica's visit, tidying up the yard and ensuring Pancake was particularly charming. The farm, nestled in the rolling hills of the countryside, was a picturesque haven filled with lush greenery and the sweet scent of wildflowers dancing in the gentle breeze. The sprawling fields stretched out before me, dotted with vibrant patches of clover and the occasional burst of colour from blooming daisies.

As I waited for her arrival, a mix of anticipation and anxiety coursed through me. What if things didn't go as I hoped? What if the distance between us was too great to bridge? I shook off the doubts, focusing instead on the warmth of the sun and the rustling of leaves in the trees that framed the property.

When Jessica finally hopped out of the taxi, her smile was infectious. "This place is amazing!" she exclaimed, taking in the sights with wide eyes. The wooden farmhouse, with its quaint stone façade and cheerful blue shutters, stood proudly against the backdrop of a brilliant sky, while a cobblestone path wound its way through the garden, leading to the front door. I couldn't help but grin back, feeling a sense of pride as I showed her around.

We wandered through the farm, stopping to feed the pigs and laugh at their antics. The pigpen, a lively space filled with mud and straw, was home to a merry band of pigs, who squealed and snorted as they jostled for the best treats. Pancake, the rotund little creature I had come to adore, trotted over with her tail wagging, snuffling at Jessica's shoes and prompting a fit of giggles from her.

"Look at her! She's like a little tank!" Jessica laughed, crouching down to give Pancake a scratch behind the ears. The warmth of her laughter echoed in the air, and for the first time in months, it felt like we were slipping back into our old rhythm, the joy of our shared moments flowing more freely than it had in ages.

After spending time with the pigs, we made our way over to the sheep paddock, where fluffy white clouds of wool grazed lazily on the grass. The sheep, with their soft bleating and gentle demeanour, added a tranquil feel to the farm. I watched as Jessica crouched down to get a closer look, her eyes lighting up at the sight of a particularly curious lamb that ambled over to investigate.

"This is idyllic!" she said, her voice filled with awe. "I can't believe you get to live here!"

"I know," I replied, a sense of pride swelling within me. "It's peaceful, and the animals really do make it special."

As we sat on the grass, surrounded by the gentle sounds of nature, I felt a sense of calm settle over me. The sun slipped lower in the sky, casting a warm golden glow across the fields. "I've missed this," I admitted, my voice soft. "I've missed you."

Jessica looked at me, her expression thoughtful. "I've missed you too. College has been… overwhelming. I didn't realise how much I needed a break from all that. This is nice."

The air between us felt charged, and I couldn't help but wonder if this was the moment I had been waiting for—the chance to reclaim the connection we had lost. The farm, with its idyllic charm, vibrant flowers, and gentle animals, felt like the perfect backdrop for our rekindled love.

The Edge of Darkness

THREE

As the sun dipped below the horizon, casting long shadows across the farm, a darker thought began to swirl in my mind, sending a cold shiver down my spine. I had felt a flicker of something unsettling, an electric rush of adrenaline that surged through me as I stared at Jessica, her laughter echoing in my ears. The warmth of our reunion was slowly overshadowed by a growing resentment that I could no longer ignore.

The moments we had shared, filled with joy and laughter, were now tainted by the months of distance and neglect. I felt a deep ache in my chest, a mixture of longing and anger twisting into something far darker. How could she just abandon me for her new friends? It was as if she had turned her back on everything we had built together, and the sting of betrayal cut deeper than I had anticipated.

In that moment, I realised I wanted her to understand the weight of her choices. I wanted her to feel the agony of my loneliness, to grasp the depth of my hurt. The thought of punishing her for the time she had stolen from me began to enthral me, an intoxicating idea that sent adrenaline coursing through my veins like fire.

My mind raced back to the knife I had left at home, its blade gleaming with a menacing allure that had transformed it from a playful tool into a sinister weapon in my imagination. What if I used it to teach her a lesson? The notion was exhilarating, a dark fantasy that felt both terrifying and groping. I could envision it clearly—the blade glinting under the moonlight, the rush of power that would surge through me as I made her confront the consequences of her choices.

As we walked back to the pigpen, I watched Jessica twisting and twirling her hair, a chill ran through me. The image of her face, once so bright and full of life, twisted into something darker in my mind. Would she finally understand the depths of my pain if she were forced to confront it? Would she see how profoundly I loved her, and how deeply I had suffered in her absence?

I pushed the thoughts away, shaking my head as if to rid myself of the darkness creeping in. Yet they lingered, tempting me with their seductive allure. I felt a battle within me—a struggle between the part that craved her love and the part that yearned for revenge.

The farm, once a place of solace, now felt like a battleground for my internal conflict. The gentle sounds of the animals faded into the background, replaced by the pounding of my heart as I wrestled with the urge to act on my darker impulses. I knew this wasn't who I was, but the pain of rejection twisted my thoughts into something unrecognisable.

As I glanced at Jessica, her back turned to me as she crouched to pet Pancake again, I felt a surge of emotions—

anger, betrayal, longing—swirling together in a chaotic storm. I wanted to reach out, to pull her close and remind her of the love we shared. But that yearning was overshadowed by the darker thoughts that beckoned me closer, whispering promises of power and control.

The knife at home became an obsession, a symbol of the twisted path my mind was wandering down. I imagined holding it, the cold metal pressing against my palm, the weight of it heavy with terrifying possibilities as I confronted her with the truth of my feelings.

In that moment, I knew I was teetering on the edge of a precipice, caught between the desire for connection and the urge to lash out.

As the sky darkened and the stars began to twinkle overhead, I realised I was at a crossroads. The choice lay before me, and the path I took would irrevocably change everything. With a heart full of turmoil and a mind clouded by rage, I had to decide whether to embrace the darkness or seek the light once more. The thrill of the unknown tugged at me, a siren's call that promised power, control, and perhaps, in some twisted way, a chance to reclaim the love I had lost.

"Shall we head back?" Jessica asks, her beautiful red lips trembling like a leaf in the wind. "I'm absolutely frozen!"

"Of course! Let's retreat to the warmth of my lair," I reply with a cheeky grin. "We can indulge in some classic shenanigans, just like the good old days!"

With the farm not too far a walk away from home, we set off, me draping my heavy metal band hoodie over her shoulders like a makeshift blanket. It was a proper rock 'n' roll number, emblazoned with skulls and fire, and I could already picture her face lighting up when she saw it. "You know I've got impeccable taste in music and fashion!" I tease, winking at her.

"Oh, fabulous! Now I can look like a metal goddess while freezing my bits off!" she laughs, playfully nudging me with her shoulder. "What a look!"

As we walked, I couldn't help but joke about the absurdity of our situation. "Just think, if we were in a horror film right now, we'd definitely be the first to go. 'Two idiots walking in the dark with terrible fashion choices!'"

"Speak for yourself! I'm rocking this hoodie!" she retorted, striking a pose as if we were on a catwalk. "Just call me the queen of the undead!"

We both burst into laughter, the sound echoing through the chilly night air. With each step, the cold seemed to fade a little, replaced by the warmth of our banter.

My parents had been off gallivanting for a few days, leaving the house emptier than my social calendar. As we stepped inside, the silence was deafening—my brother had finally fled the nest. I couldn't help but feel a touch of melancholy at the thought of not hearing him rage-quit yet another video game or my mother bellowing, "Ryan, shut the fuck up! I'm trying to watch Corrie!"

But alas, he'd found his voice (and a fair few memes) and had packed his bags to live with his friends in a different town. Apparently, his "passion" for video games had blossomed into a full-blown career, and he'd set up his own YouTube channel, raking in royalties like some sort of digital overlord. Pathetic? More like a legend in his own lunchtime!

I mean, who knew that sitting in your pants, shouting at a screen, could actually pay off? Meanwhile, I was left here, stuck with the echoes of his gaming tantrums and my mother's relentless soap opera critiques. I sighed dramatically, imagining him sitting in his new flat, surrounded by empty takeout containers, blissfully unaware that the real world existed beyond his screen. What a time to be alive!

"It hasn't changed much, has it?" Jessica chuckled, her stunning green eyes flitting around the living room like a curious cat. The place had all the warmth of a sterile hospital, thanks to my mother's obsessive cleaning habits. I half-expected to find a surgeon waiting in the corner, ready to scrub in.

"Nope, Mum is still absolutely bonkers!" I shot back, laughing as I gestured for her to follow me. "Come on, let's escape this sanitised prison!"

As we climbed the stairs, my mind was a chaotic whirlpool of thoughts—should I charm her with my witticisms or lure her into my lair with something a bit more sinister? The idea of both sent a shiver of excitement down my spine. What if I could sweep her off her feet, then turn the evening into a thrilling escapade where we'd either lose ourselves in passion or descend into delightful madness?

I pushed open my bedroom door, revealing a space that was slightly less clean—more like a controlled chaos, with clothes strewn about like casualties of a fashion war. "Welcome to my den of iniquity!" I declared with a flourish, my heart racing at the possibilities. "Take your pick: we could binge-watch horror films, or I could give you a guided tour of my questionable life choices."

Jessica smirked, her eyes twinkling with mischief. "I'm all for a bit of chaos. What's the plan, then? Seduction or sinister surprises?"

"Why not both?" I said with a grin, the thrill of the night pulsing through me as I took a step closer, the air thick with tension and unspoken desires. This was going to be one hell of an evening.

I turn to Jessica, my eyes roaming over every exquisite detail of her figure, each curve igniting a wildfire of thoughts in my mind. With a mixture of confidence and anticipation, I step closer, my hands steady as I reach for the hem of my hoodie she was wearing..

As I lift it upward, my fingers brush against her skin, sending a thrill through me as I outline the contours of her body. She had been shivering earlier, but that was to be expected—beautiful Jessica was the kind of girl who thrived on defiance, her choice of attire a testament to her bold spirit. Clad in nothing but a skimpy black vest, no bra, she radiated an effortless allure that was impossible to ignore. She was always impossible to ignore.

Sure, she might have changed in some ways, but her daring fashion sense and that tantalising figure remained utterly unchanged. A wicked grin spreads across my face as I take in the sight before me, feeling the air thicken with unspoken tension. This moment was electric, charged with possibilities.

'I am going to fuck every single inch of you' I lick my lips as I carry on undressing this beautiful being in front of me. A pair of full, rounded mounds rise gracefully from her chest, her smooth, velvety skin glistening softly under the dull bedroom light, reminiscent of ripe peaches beckoning for attention, my attention. Each nipple stands as a delicate pink bud, slightly protruding, drawing the eye with an irresistible allure. The gentle curve of her areola frames it like a perfect halo, accentuating her beauty in a way that feels almost sacred, I fucking love this girl, how dare she have changed so much. With the faintest movement, they sway enticingly, a dance of temptation that leaves a lingering promise in the air, inviting further exploration and igniting a spark of desire that is impossible to ignore.

Jessica's face turns into a face full of passion, biting her lip for added beauty. I plunge my hand down her leggings, no knickers either.

As I began, my fingertips grazed her outer pussy, tracing delicate patterns that sent shivers of warmth through her. I could feel her sensitivity awaken under my touch, the wetness unleashing, urging me to explore further. Gradually, I applied more pressure, teasing the entrance with gentle strokes, keenly observing her reactions to find out what brought her pleasure.

With a rhythmic motion, I curled my fingers, matching her natural contours, varying my speed and pressure to keep the sensation heightened. I focused on her clit, drawing gentle circles and light flicks, creating waves of pleasure that seemed to resonate throughout her body and through the light moans she was letting out. I stayed attuned to her responses, adjusting my movements to enhance her enjoyment, feeling the connection deepen. This exploration was exhilarating, and I could sense the unspoken craving for more between us. I pull out my fingers and lick them, tasting her juices, this let out the animal in her and just like that, she throws me back onto the bed.

'Can we use the knife? Or some candles? I'm feeling pretty carried away Dahlia, do whatever you fucking want to me right now!' Jessica's perfect moans slipped from her precious mouth.

The air crackled with deep electric tension as I grasped the knife, its blade catching the dim bedroom light in a way that felt sinister. Jessica's emerald eyes widened, a mixture of fear and exhilaration flickering across her face. She asked me to do this The thrill of the moment surged within me, intoxicating and dangerous. Just how I loved to live my life.

"Dahlia, what are you doing?" she gasped, her voice trembling as she tries to sit up, but my mind was racing, consumed by a desire to reclaim the power that had slipped through my fingers, fuck the safe words, the world is my oyster right here, right now.

In a reckless whirl of emotions, I moved closer, driven by an unrelenting urge to push boundaries, nothing would stop me. "I want to feel something real, something raw," I whispered, my heart pounding in my chest. The thrill had morphed into a dangerous game, one I was all too willing to play to satisfy my need for adrenaline.

Before I could think, I pressed the blade against her flawless thigh, just enough to break the surface of her skin. The sharpness elicited a gasp from her lips, her eyes further widening in shock. "Dahlia, no!" she screamed, but the sound was drowned out by the adrenaline coursing through my veins. I'm not stopping, not ever.

With a swift, deliberate motion, I sliced deeper, the knife gliding through flesh with a sickening sound. Jessica's scream pierced the air, a raw, sound that sent a chill down my spine. It was both terrifying and exhilarating, a rush that ignited something dark and powerful.

"Why are you doing this?" she cried, her voice laced with anguish as she clutched her thigh, blood seeping between her fingers. The sight of her pain was intoxicating, a dangerous cocktail of fear and power.

"I need you to understand!" I shouted, the weight of my actions crashing over me like a tidal wave. "You left me! You abandoned everything we had, and I wanted you to feel the intensity of what I'm capable of!"

As her eyes filled with tears, I saw the flicker of fear transform into something else—defiance. She gritted her teeth, determination shining through the pain. "This isn't love, Dahlia! You're losing yourself!"

"Jessica, I..." I faltered, the knife trembling in my hand as my heart raced.

The pain etched on her face was a huge reminder of the fragile line between love and obsession. "You need to fix this," she gasped, her breath coming in ragged bursts. "You need to choose—this darkness or me."

"I choose the darkness'

"Why are you doing this?" she cried, her voice filled with anguish as she clutched her thigh, blood seeping between her fingers. The sight of her pain was intoxicating, a vile cocktail of fear and power that surged through me like a drug.

"I need you to understand!" I shouted, the weight of my actions crashing over me like a relentless storm. "You left me! You abandoned everything we had, and I wanted you to feel the intensity of what I'm capable of!"

As her eyes filled with tears, I saw the flicker of fear transform into something else—defiance. She gritted her teeth, determination shining through the pain. "This isn't love, Dahlia! You're losing yourself!"

"I said I choose the darkness!" The words tasted bitter on my tongue, but they resonated with a twisted sense of liberation. In that moment, I felt the protection of my previous self shatter, leaving only a void where love once thrived. "You think I don't know what I'm doing?" I sneered, stepping closer, relishing the fear that danced in her eyes. "You've pushed me to this. You've made me this way."

She shook her head, desperate. "Dahlia, you're losing your mind, you're insane! This isn't who you are!"

But I loved the darkness wrapping around me like an embrace, whispering sweet nothings in my ear. "This is who I am now. You've turned me into this, Jessica. You and your slutty ways."

"Please," she whimpered, her beautiful gaze faltering as her fear took over. "You don't have to do this. We can still find a way back, I'll, I'll stop college!."

"Find a way back?" I laughed, an authentic laugh. "There's no going back from this. You've stripped away every piece of me that cared. Now, I'm free."

Her eyes widened beautifully filled with a mix of horror and disbelief. "You're making a fucking big mistake, Dahlia. This will only ruin you."

"Let it fucking destroy me," I spat venom. "If I can't have you and just you, I will strive in this beautiful darkness."

With each word, I felt the exhilaration swell within me, a power I'd never known before. The knife dripped in crimson, a perfected reflection of the monster I had become. I stepped closer, the air thick with a tension that felt better than fucking Jessica with my fingers.

"Dahlia..." she gasped, her voice trembling, a sound that was only falling onto deaf ears.

But it was too late. It was over. The darkness had claimed me, and I welcomed it with wide open arms. I plunged the knife deeper, not just into her, but into the last seconds of my own humanity. In that moment, I knew the real Dahlia was now lost. There would be no happy ending —only the twisted satisfaction of power and the haunting echoes of what once was of Jessica. Stab, thrust, strike. I watched the perfectly disrobed Jessica lay there.

Oh, I felt an overwhelming sense of isolation, as if the very air around me had thickened with dimness. The world outside continued on, blissfully unaware of the horror that had unfolded within these bedroom walls. I could almost hear the distant sounds of life outside, laughter, music, the chatter of people going about their days, albeit drunk, were they mocking me?

As I knelt beside Jessica, the intense warmth of her cherry blood staining my fingers, I watched it pool around her, a dark scarlet sea that contrasted sharply against the pale beige carpeted floor, mum would kill me if she saw the mess. Each laboured breath she took was a reminder of her life slipping away, a beautiful affirmation of my triumph over her, I had won. I had wanted her to understand my pain.

"Why did it have to come to this?" I spat in her face, the words dripping with malice, as if her very existence had irritated me. I reached out, my fingers trembling as they brushed against her skin, now colder than the night air. The stark contrast between her once-vibrant self and the lifeless form before me sent amazing satisfaction through my veins.

The darkness enveloped me, a suffocating shroud that whispered promises of power and freedom. I was no longer bound by the shackles of jealousy, I had unleashed the true Dahlia, a creature of destruction.

"Look at what you've made me," I murmured, my voice barely above a whisper.. "You pushed me to this point, Jessica. You left me no choice."

The knife lay discarded on the floor, a proud emblem to my madness, and I felt a perverse thrill at the thought of what I had done. I had transformed from a mere shadow of myself into something far more sinister..

As I stood, the room felt tremendously alive.. I could almost hear the walls whispering my name, clapping and then beckoning me deeper into the abyss. The thrill of my actions resonated within me—this was liberation untied from the chains that had held me captive for far too long.

I stared down at Jessica, her lifeless body now a grotesque canvas of my rage.

A wicked smile crept across my lips as I contemplated the life I had stolen. I had become the creator of my own destruction, a mistress of the night. As I turned away from her, I felt the weight of her absence settle on my shoulders, a trophy I would carry into the depths of my new existence.

The world outside continued to spin, blissfully unaware of the darkness that now resided within me and as I walked away, the echoes of Jessica's laughter haunted me, mingling with the thrill of what just occurred.

I took my descent down the stairs, the wood mum had polished creaking dramatically beneath my feet like it was auditioning for a part in my very own horror movie. Ironic I know. The house was eerily quiet, quieter than ever before but there was an amazing feeling in the air. The dull hum of the fridge filled the silence, a constant reminder that life carried on, for me at least

Entering the kitchen, I flicked on the kettle, the steam rushing out like it was trying to escape the awkwardness of the moment, filled with all my secrets. I moved with a strange mix of urgency and calm as I grabbed my favourite mug—a simple white ceramic, cracked but still standing strong with the letter D embraced in flowers, Dahlias of course. Jessica brought me this mug several months back. Making coffee felt like a normal thing to do, a way to pretend everything was just fine, I mean it was fine, more than fine now.

As the kettle boiled, my mind raced with several thoughts all bickering with one another. Where was I going to hide Jessica's body? The panic hit me like a cold splash of iced water. What would I say to her family? I could already picture the looks of horror on their faces, and it made my stomach twist uncomfortably. "Oh, Jessica? Yeah she's just taking an extended holiday!" I imagined myself saying, forcing a grin.

The kettle clicked off with a dramatised suddenness that made me jump, and I poured the hot water over the coffee grounds, breathing in the rich aroma, coffee is equally as exhilarating as killing someone. It was a warm hug that sought no answers, but that panic was still there, mildly lurking. I stirred the perfect blend of coffee, milk and two sugars, watching the dark liquid swirl from black to brown. It was a perfect metaphor for my brain right now—dark and slightly sweet

With my steaming cup in hand, I leaned against the counter, feeling the warmth seep into me. I took a sip, the sweet taste hitting my tongue, and for a moment, I felt like a master criminal.

The panic bubbled within me, reminding me I needed a plan and that plan needed to come quick. I couldn't just leave her lying around; the house was too small, too familiar and oh, my family would return soon. My mind raced through ideas, each one more ridiculous than the last. "Maybe I can stuff her in the wardrobe?" I thought, and then quickly shook my head at my naïve little brain.

Meat The Problem

FOUR

....

As I stood in the kitchen, cradling my steaming cup of coffee, a wild thought crossed my mind: feeding Jessica to the pigs. It was a plan that had a certain dark charm to it, albeit a rather gruesome one. Pigs were famously known as efficient eaters, and I couldn't help but chuckle at the strangeness of it all. "Who knew I'd end up with such a piggy problem?" I muttered to myself, taking another sip of coffee.

The idea took root in my mind, and soon enough, I was mentally drafting my plan. First things first: I needed to craft a believable story for her family. "Oh, Jessica? She's off on a spontaneous retreat in the countryside!" I imagined telling them, trying to keep a straight face. "You know her, always looking to connect with nature." I could almost hear their responses, full of concern and confusion, but I'd play the role of the supportive friend, reassuring them it was all perfectly normal.

Next, I decided I needed to put my plans in writing. I rummaged through my desk drawer and pulled out an assortment of colourful sticky notes and scrap paper. "Why not make this a bit more organised?" I thought, chuckling at the ridiculousness of my situation. I began jotting down my ideas, each note a piece of my twisted puzzle.

Note 1: "Feed Jessica to the pigs." Simple enough.

Note 2: "Tell her family she's went away." That one required a bit of flair, I thought.

Note 3: "Ensure no one is home when I do it." Always a sensible precaution!

As I scribbled and scribbled away, I couldn't help but feel excited with the thought of my little notes piling up. I tucked them away in different spots throughout my room—one under the bed, another in the back of my sock drawer, and a particularly cheeky one inside my favourite novel, where I could pretend it was just another layer of my literary taste. "I'll be the world's worst author if this ever gets published," I laughed darkly to myself.

I made sure to keep everything discreet, knowing that if anyone stumbled upon my notes, it would raise eyebrows, or worse, lead to questions. "Just a little reminder to myself," I'd say if confronted, flashing an innocent smile. "You know how it is—life gets hectic!"

With my notes hidden, I felt a strange sense of calm wash over me. I had a plan, albeit a humorous one, and it was almost comforting to think I was taking control of the situation. The pigs would do the work for me, and I'd be left with just the memory of Jessica, which I could spin into a story for her family when they came asking. Genius.

I needed to think of a better plan than Jessica running off to the countryside.

New Plan: "The Model Dream"

The tale unfolds like this: "Oh, Jessica? She's off to pursue her dream of becoming a model abroad!" I would explain, trying to keep my tone casual, as if this was all perfectly normal. "We went to that concert on Sunday, and she got scouted by this big-shot talent agent right there in the crowd! Can you believe it?"

I'd go on to add "The weirdo agent was absolutely taken with her and offered to pay for her flights and accommodation. She was so excited! He wanted to whisk her away that same day. I tried to talk her out of it, really I did! But she was determined. You know how she gets when she has her mind set on something."

Then, I'd add a sincere touch, "I promised her I'd keep you all happy while she's away. I told her I'd keep in touch, and I would make sure to update you on everything when I can!"

To make the story even more believable, I'd mention how Jessica left her phone behind in the rush to leave, which had really panicked me. "I was worried sick at first, thinking she might need to reach out or that something was wrong! But then I realised she was just so caught up in the moment that she forgot!" I'd say, trying to sound convincing.

This would give her family a reason to stay in touch, asking about Jessica's new adventure, and it would help distract them from the truth. The sheer excitement of her unexpected modelling opportunity would overshadow their concerns, buying me some much-needed time to execute this eccentric plan while maintaining the façade of being a supportive friend.

As I stood there, the weight of my secret pressed heavily on my chest. Jessica was gone, and while the world would mourn for her, I felt that thrill coursing through me. I had orchestrated her demise, and now, I was left with the remnants of a plan that I know will go exactly as I intended.

The story I needed to craft wouldn't just be about her absence; it would be a twisted tale of adventure that would keep everyone distracted from the truth. I could almost hear her voice, that irritatingly bright tone, as I recalled how she had rushed off, so naïve and eager for that modelling opportunity. I could shape her legacy in a way that suited me.

Ensuring Jessica's body was disposed of without a hitch was crucial. I had a secluded spot at the farm, cleverly tucked away behind a thicket of bushes—ideal for my purposes. Out of sight but close enough to the pigs, who I was certain would appreciate an unexpected midnight snack. I could already picture them, tails wagging with glee, ready for their surprise feast. "Pigs are just big, happy waste disposal units," I chuckled to myself, grinning at the thought of the headlines that would never be written: "Local Pigs Feast on Runaway Model—Only in This Town!"

As night fell, I gathered my tools, lining up everything I would need: a large tarp, some heavy-duty garbage bags, and a shovel, thank god my father had an array of supplies for the farm, our families safe place. I felt like a darkly comedic character in a twisted play, preparing for the ultimate punchline.

Under the cloak of darkness, I made my move. I started at the house, where everything had unfolded. The cool night air sent a shiver down my spine, but it wasn't from fear—it was the thrill of the secret I was about to carry out. I carefully dragged Jessica's lifeless form from the room, wrapping her in the tarp with meticulous care, as if preparing a bizarre gift for the pigs.

As I stepped outside, I hoisted the bundle over my shoulder, the weight both exhilarating and surreal. "Let's take a little stroll, shall we?" I said aloud to no one, heading down the winding path that led to the pig pen. The moon hung low in the sky, casting a silvery glow over the countryside, illuminating my path as crickets serenaded the night.

Each step felt like a scene from a dark comedy, the absurdity of the situation making me chuckle. "You know, Jessica, if you had just stayed put, we wouldn't be in this mess. But here we are, a glamorous model and her loyal friend, taking a late-night hike through the countryside!" I laughed to myself, imagining the headlines that would never come: "Local Woman Takes Her Friend for a Walk—Only to Feed Her to Pigs!"

I led Jessica behind a patch of soil, where the ground was soft and dark—a perfect spot for the next phase of my plan. With a wicked grin, I laid her down and pulled out my tools, feeling like a butcher about to create a culinary masterpiece.

As I set to work, I couldn't help but think of the practicality of it all. Pigs can eat anything but hair and bones, but hair can be burned, and bones ground up to make fertiliser. "Talk about recycling!" I muttered, chuckling at the absurdity of my situation.

With careful precision, I cut Jessica into portions with my fathers favourite cleaver, my heart racing with each slice. The darkness concealed my actions, and the thrill of it all gave me a rush. I placed the pieces into heavy-duty garbage bags, each one filled with the remnants of my former friend. "This is what you get for crossing me," I joked, while the pigs continued to snuffle around, blissfully unaware of the feast that would soon be theirs.

Once I had everything neatly packed away, I shoved the bags into a suitcase that father had left in the shed after one night he stayed amongst the animals. It felt absurdly mundane, as if I were preparing for a weekend getaway instead of a gruesome disposal. "Just heading to a friend's house, nothing to see here!" I said, stifling a laugh.

With everything in place, I decided to call a taxi to the farm. I dialled the number, trying to sound casual. "Hi, yes, I need a taxi to pick me up at the farm. Just heading to stay at a friend's house!!" I finished, my voice full of forged nonchalance.

As I hung up, I couldn't help but think about the pigs and what a delight they would have. "Enjoy the buffet, my friends!" I called out, waving goodbye to Jessica's remains as I prepared to leave. I felt giddy at the thought of all of this, a darkly humorous twist in a story that was only just beginning.

With the taxi pulling up, I took one last look at the farm, the night air electric with excitement. "Let's make sure this stays our little secret," I whispered, stepping into the vehicle, suitcase in hand and a wicked grin on my face, it's as if I want to be caught!

Whispers In The Park

FIVE

As I settled into the present, my mind wandered back to that fateful night—a time when I had transformed from a mere bystander in life to the orchestrator of my own dark comedy. The thrill of that experience still sent shivers down my spine, even a decade later. I had learned much since then, honing my craft in the art of subtle manipulation and the delicious exhilaration of orchestrating another's downfall.

My initial encounter with my new prey had been at the local café, a quaint little spot that boasted the best pastries in town. I remembered the day vividly. The bell above the door chimed as she stepped in, sunlight spilling over her like a golden halo. She was radiant, with wild red hair that bounced as she walked and bright green eyes that sparkled with curiosity, eyes like Jessica's.. I had been behind the counter, my usual demeanour charming and welcoming, but inside, I was already sizing her up.

She approached the counter, her gaze flitting over the menu, and I realised this was my chance to observe her more closely. "What can I get for you today?" I asked, my smile warm and inviting.

"I'll have a large caramel macchiato, please," she replied, her voice a perfect melody to my ears. "And one of those chocolate croissants."

I nodded, noting the way her face lit up at the mention of the croissant—a small, indulgent treat that seemed to match her vibrant spirit. As I prepared her order, I couldn't help but steal glances in her direction. She chatted animatedly with her friends, laughter bubbling from her like a fountain of joy. It was infectious, and I felt a tingle of excitement at the thought of her becoming part of my life, even if only for a brief moment.

After I handed her the steaming cup and the flaky pastry, she flashed me a dazzling smile, completely unaware of the shadows lurking behind my eyes. "Thanks! I'll definitely be back for more!" she said, before turning and joining her friends at a nearby table. That was the moment the gears began turning in my mind; I had to keep her close, observe her habits, and find the right moment to strike.

Fast forward a few weeks, and there I was again, lounging in the park, the sun casting a warm glow over the lush green grass. I had taken on a lot of overtime at the café and seemed to be always there when she visited. I often watched her, blending into the background, reading a book or sipping coffee, always careful to maintain the guise of the helpful barista.

Now, sitting on a weathered bench beneath a sprawling oak tree, I reflected on how I had been captivated by her charm from that very first encounter. She was a creature of habit, always arriving at the same time, settling on a vibrant picnic blanket with that same radiant smile. Her laughter rang out like music, completely unaware of the darkness lurking in my heart. It was almost comical how closely she resembled Jessica, my former friend, as if fate had served her up to me on a silver platter, garnished with a side of irony.

I leaned back on the bench, a wicked grin creeping onto my face. "Oh, darling, you have no idea what's coming, do you?" I muttered under my breath, watching her interact with her friends, blissfully ignorant of the impending doom. The thrill of the hunt surged through me, igniting memories of that night with Jessica—how I had artfully sliced and diced, feeding her remains to the pigs, all while chuckling at the absurdity of it all.

As I observed my prey, I couldn't help but dream up elaborate plans. Perhaps I could convince her to embark on a weekend adventure, just like I had done with Jessica. "We'll have so much fun, just the two of us," I could say, my voice dripping with sugary sweetness. It would be simple yet effective: lure her away from her safety net, create a diversion, and then execute my dark vision under the cover of night.

The park was alive with activity, the sound of laughter mingling with the dulcet tones of a nearby saxophonist playing Ed Sheeran. I imagined the perfect scenario—a secluded spot beneath the trees, a patch of soft earth where the soil would eagerly absorb any evidence. I could almost hear the pigs snorting in anticipation once again, their delight at the feast I would provide. "They can eat anything but hair and bones," I chuckled to myself, "but hair can be burned, and bones ground up to make fertiliser. Talk about a green initiative!" I always say this to myself before capturing my prey.

The girl glanced my way for a brief moment, a smile lighting up her face, and my heart raced with excitement. I smiled back, feigning innocence. "Oh, sweet girl," I thought, "you have no idea how effortlessly you'll become part of my end."

As I continued to watch her, I relished the absurdity of the situation. Here I was, a charming figure in a park, surrounded by joyous families and playful dogs, plotting the next chapter of my twisted tale. The park buzzed with life, yet I felt a dark thrill pulsing through me, a delicious secret that set me apart from the cheerfulness around me.

"Perhaps we could enjoy a lovely picnic together," I mused, imagining her delight as I laid out a spread of gourmet snacks—only for her to discover that my idea of a picnic included a much darker twist. I could envision her laughing, completely unaware that I was preparing for her a banquet of my own design.

With each passing moment, the anticipation built within me. This was only the beginning. Just like Jessica and the other girls, this girl would soon find herself ensnared in my web—another chapter in my wicked story. And as I watched her frolic with her friends, I couldn't help but think about the pigs

In that moment, the park felt like a stage, and I was both an audience member and the director, eagerly awaiting the curtain to rise on my next act. The sun dipped lower in the sky, casting long shadows that danced like spectres, hinting at the darkness that lay just beneath the surface of this seemingly idyllic scene. And with a chuckle, I settled in, ready to watch the unfolding spectacle of life, death, and the absurdity that came with it all.

My parents had died just before my 19th birthday, leaving me to navigate a world that felt cold and unforgiving. My father, once a sharp-suited businessman, had turned to farming in search of a simpler, more fulfilling life. My mother, on the other hand, was a whirlwind of chaos—obsessed with her soap operas and perpetually shouting at the television as if her life depended on it. When they passed, it felt as if the light had been snuffed out.

Before they died, my father's suspicions began to grow, especially regarding the pigs. It started innocently enough, with a few animals disappearing now and then—nothing unusual in the farming world. But as time went on, he noticed the herd was becoming suspiciously fat, and the replacements never quite matched the originals. "Why do I keep needing to replace these pigs?" he would mutter to himself, scratching his head in confusion. I couldn't help but stifle a laugh. It was like a tragic comedy unfolding right before my eyes.

And then there were the bonfires. Oh, how he would frown and peer out of the window, watching the flames dance in the night sky. "What in the world is she burning out there?" he'd wonder aloud, glancing at me with a mixture of concern and curiosity. Each time I lit a fire in the fields, it was a necessary part of my process—a way to dispose of the remnants of my darker activities. But to him, it was just another quirk of his increasingly strange daughter. "Must be another one of her 'art projects,'" he'd say with a sigh, shaking his head as if I were some misunderstood artist.

Then came the bone shredder. I couldn't help but chuckle at the thought of how many times he'd had to replace it. "What on earth do you need that for?" he'd ask, raising an eyebrow as I feigned innocence, claiming it was for the leftover scraps from the farm. "Just making sure the soil stays enriched!" I'd say with a bright smile, not revealing that the real reason was far more sinister. After all, what's a little bone meal between family?

As I sat on the weathered bench, lost in my thoughts, the red haired girl approached me. Her vibrant red hair caught the sunlight, cascading around her shoulders like a fiery halo. She had a warm smile that seemed to light up the area, and I felt a flutter of excitement in my chest.

"Hi, I'm Bella," she said, her voice sweet and inviting. "I noticed you sitting here alone. Mind if I join you?"

"Not at all," I replied, a charming smile spreading across my face. "I'm Dahlia. I see you often at the café and here, you're fucking beautiful. I've always wondered though, do you like animals?"

Bella's eyes sparkled with curiosity. "I love them! I used to volunteer at a local animal shelter."

"Perfect! I have a farm just outside of town. You should come visit sometime. I have plenty of animals to show you," I suggested, my mind racing with possibilities.

Her enthusiasm matched my own, and I could already picture her laughter mingling with the sounds of the farm.

After scribbling down Bella's number on a crumpled piece of paper, I find myself perched on this park bench, the world around me slowly fading into the background. The sun hangs low in the sky, casting a lovely golden hue over the trees, while a gentle breeze rustles the leaves. Honestly, it's like a scene from a rom-com, minus the over-the-top music and quirky best friend who always seems to pop up at the worst moments.

I can't help but picture an evening with Bella, one that feels almost too vivid to be just a daydream. I imagine us in a quaint little farmhouse on the farm, the air thick with the scent of hay. Bella's laughter rings out, playful and bright, as she tosses straw in my direction like we're in some sort of agricultural battle. Her eyes sparkle with mischief—probably plotting her next move to distract me while she escapes..

As I sit there, I envision our playful banter giving way to something deeper. I picture myself reaching out to tuck a strand of hair behind her ear, our fingers brushing together. It's a romantic gesture, until I accidentally poke her in the eye. "Sorry!" I'd stammer, trying to recover my dignity while she giggles at my utter clumsiness.

In this whimsical daydream, the barn transforms into a place where we can explore our connection—not the place of all my victims.or at least find a good spot to hide from the rest of the world (and the new Peanut, a tremendously cute pig called Jeff, who's taken a liking to my shoelaces). I imagine the warmth of her skin against mine, although I'm pretty sure I'd get hay fever and start sneezing uncontrollably instead.

As I sit on that park bench, I let my thoughts wander further, envisioning laughter and whispered secrets filling the air, along with the occasional "What's that smell?" as we try to figure out if it's the hay or one of the local sheep. There's a bizarre sense of freedom in this fantasy, a feeling of belonging that wraps around me like a warm blanket— albeit one that's slightly itchy and covered in straw. I can think romantically can't I? But I know what lies ahead for this precious Bella.

The sky gradually darkens, I've been on this bench for ages now but my mind continues to paint vivid scenes of hilarity and connection. With every passing moment, the thought of Bella lingers, reminding me of the potential for a truly entertaining adventure. And as I hold her number in my hand, I can't help but feel a rush of excitement at the possibilities waiting just around the corner. I'll fuck her then kill, just like I had all my girls.

With thoughts of Bella swirling in my head like a particularly frothy cappuccino, I make my way back to my flat. It's not much—a cheap and dull little apartment that could easily be mistaken for a set from a low-budget sitcom. The walls are a washed-out beige, the kind that says "I'm functional but not too inviting," and the flickering fluorescent lights do little to improve the atmosphere.

As I enter, I'm greeted by the slightly musty smell of old carpet and whatever that mysterious stain on the kitchen counter is. My furniture is a mismatched collection of hand-me-downs and thrift store finds. The armchair, a faded blue monstrosity, has seen better days—probably in a different decade entirely. But it's mine, and I've grown oddly fond of its lumpy cushions and questionable support.

I sink into the armchair, a smile creeping across my face as I picture Bella's laughter. It's a bit like sinking into a cloud of mediocrity, but after a long day of steaming milk and serving lattes, it's as comfy as can be and the park had given me some sort of sensory overload. I grab my mobile phone, its cracked screen a badge of honour from countless encounters with my less-than-graceful lifestyle.

With a mix of excitement and nervousness, I dial Bella's number, my thumb hovering over the call button for a moment. It feels like I'm about to launch a space mission instead of just ringing a girl I barely know. "Come on, Dahlia, just press it!" I mutter to myself, shaking off the jitters.

Finally, I hit the button, and the phone begins to ring. I lean back in my armchair, trying to play it cool while my heart races. The sound of the ringing fills the dull silence of my apartment, and I can't help but grin like a fool. Thoughts of my future kill dance around my mind, like a montage from a rom-com where everything goes hilariously wrong but still ends up right, for me at least.

"Please pick up, please pick up," I whisper, half-expecting some miracle to happen. But instead, it's just me and the sound of my cheap wallpaper peeling in the background. My apartment may be drab, but at least I've got Bella's number, and that's a start, right? Fucking answer, I've not felt adrenaline for a while, and I need it. As the ringing continues, my heart pounds in my chest like a bass drum at a festival. Then, just as I'm about to imagine Bella's voice, it clicks over to voicemail. "You've reached Bella. Leave a message!"

"Ugh, typical!" I groan, flopping back into my armchair. But desperation kicks in, and I'm not ready to give up just yet. I take a deep breath, trying to channel my inner James Bond, and dial her number again, heart racing for that rush of adrenaline.

"Come on, Bella, pick up!" I mutter, the anticipation making me feel alive. The phone rings once more, and I lean forward, determination etched on my face as I wait, hoping this time, it won't be her answering machine.

Just as I'm starting to think my phone might be cursed, Bella's voice crackles through the receiver, sounding half-asleep and utterly adorable. "Hello?" she mumbles, clearly caught off guard.

"Hey, Bella! It's me! Sorry to wake you," I say, trying to suppress my excitement. "I was wondering if you'd fancy coming over to the farm tomorrow night?"

There's a pause, and I can almost picture her squinting at the clock, trying to remember who on earth is calling her at this ungodly hour. "The farm? What's happening there? Are you planning to sacrifice a goat or something?"

"Only if the evening goes horribly wrong!" I chuckle. "But, no, just a little adventure! Fresh air, stars, and maybe a bit of mischief."

"Right. So, should I pack my wellies or my party shoes?" she replies, her tone half-serious, half-joking. I can't help but grin at her wit.

"Oh, definitely bring both! You never know when you might need to wade through mud or dance on a hay bale," I quip. "And, erm, you might want to pack some clothes. Not that you'll really need them…" I add, letting a cheeky grin spread across my face.

"Not need them? Are you trying to lure me into some weird farm cult?" she asks, her voice a mix of amusement and curiosity. "Should I be bringing snacks, or are you planning to feed me sheep?"

"Only if you're into that sort of thing!" I laugh. "Honestly, just pack something comfy and maybe leave your sense of reason at home. Trust me, it'll be an unforgettable night!"

"Unforgettable, like the time I got stuck in a tree trying to impress my mate? Sounds safe," she replies, now sounding more alert and definitely intrigued.

"Exactly! Think of it as a rural escape room—except instead of puzzles, we'll just have sheep judging our every move," I say, relishing the absurdity of it all. "And if we're lucky, we might even spot a rogue cow trying to join the party!"

"Right, so I'm basically signing up for a night of farmyard chaos. What's the catch?" she asks, her laughter bubbling through the line.

"Catch? No catch! Just good fun, fresh air, and perhaps a few questionable life choices," I say, my heart racing at the thought of our night on the farm—filled with adventure, laughter, and a touch of delightful madness.

"Alright, I'm in! But if I end up being chased by a sheep in the dead of night, I'm blaming you!" she retorts, her laughter echoing through the line.

"Deal! Just remember, if you see a sheep with a suspicious glint in its eye, run like the wind!" I reply, my excitement bubbling over.

I set the phone down, a wicked grin spreading across my face. Talking with Bella had sparked a flicker of excitement, the prospect of spending an evening together at the farm stirring something long dormant within me. As I replayed our conversation, a delightful shiver of anticipation mingled with a desperate craving for a good dose of adrenaline. This could be my end and why not make it something wonderfully twisted and unexpected.

Leaning back in my chair, I allowed darker possibilities to swirl in my mind. With Bella, I sensed an opportunity to inject some much-needed final thrill into my life, like adding a splash of Worcester sauce to a bland dish. And let's be honest, picturing her perfect body—every curve and contour—only added to the deliciously dark fantasy. It was like dreaming of dessert while on a diet; completely indulgent with just a hint of guilt. I'm going to make this final kill perfect, after all it has been three years since my last.

The weight of my previous actions loomed like a ghost at a dinner party, but perhaps it could be turned into something more entertaining. For now, I'd focus on the allure of manipulation—a chance to enjoy her company while reeling her into the shadows I'd embraced. The future felt like a tightrope act. I couldn't wait to see where this sinister path might lead, knowing full well that this night could reveal my end—and perhaps a few skeletons along the way, well perhaps not, they were well taken care of. After all, what's a little darkness without a side of humour?

As I imagine the scene that would offer, Bella's red hair cascades down her back like a fiery waterfall. Her eyes sparkle with a mix of fear and arousal as she lies on the farmhouse floor, I'd make the area nice and warm with the blanket I always used for my other victims, clean of course. My gaze is drawn to her breasts, where her nipples stand proud and inviting. They're small and pink, with a subtle sheen to them that suggests they're already sensitive.

I picture Bella's nipples responding to every touch, every whispered promise. They harden and soften in time with her ragged breathing, as if beckoning me closer. The image is intoxicating, and I feel myself becoming lost in the fantasy.

My attention drifts downward, to the curve of Bella's hips and the smooth expanse of her thighs. I imagine her pussy shaven and bare, the skin slick with moisture as she trembles with anticipation. Her lips already plump and swollen, parted slightly to reveal a hint of pink within. A thin trickle of wetness runs down from her, glistening on the smooth skin of her thighs like a promise of the pleasures to come.

As I picture Bella's body, I can almost smell the sweet scent of her arousal - a sweet smell of honey that draws me in like a magnet. Her skin is pale and smooth, with a subtle glow that hints at the passion simmering just beneath the surface. As I imagine my hands reaching out to touch her, I can almost feel the warmth of her skin, the gentle give of her flesh beneath my fingers.

The knife glints in the dim light, its presence a reminder of the danger and excitement that lurks at the heart of this fantasy. But even as fear threatens to overwhelm Bella, my attention remains fixed on her nipples - on the way they respond to every touch, every whispered promise. And below, where her shaven pussy waits like an open invitation - wet and ready for whatever comes next.

And then, in an instant, everything changes. The knife flashes downward, heading straight for Bella...I can't wait to make these thoughts to unravel out in front of me. It's been weeks since I've had my fingers inside a woman - weeks since I've felt the warm thrill of penetration or heard the sweet sounds of pleasure that come from between a woman's legs when she's being properly worshipped by another woman who knows exactly what she's doing. My own desires have been simmering just below the surface for far too long now. It's not often you find someone who shares your darker tastes but when you do... magic happens.

Leah

SIX

....

The nostalgia is almost palpable as I delve into the depths of my twisted past, revisiting the memories of my second victim, a tale that unfolded two years after the disappearance of the lovely Jessica. It's astonishing how quickly people can forget, or rather, choose to forget. Jessica's family had all but given up hope of ever seeing their beloved daughter again, convinced that she had abandoned them for the allure of modelling and a life of supposed glamour.

The last instagram post from her account, which I had so meticulously crafted, was the final blow to their dwindling hopes. It was a masterpiece, if I do say so myself - a heartfelt declaration of her disdain for her family and her eagerness to start anew with someone she loved.

The post read: "I've met someone amazing and I'm starting a new chapter in my life. I'm done with the toxic relationships and suffocating expectations. I'll never be returning home." it was almost poetic, don't you think? The way it seemed to dance on the edge of truth and deception. As I reflect on that cleverly crafted post, a sense of pride still swells within me. It was a masterpiece of manipulation, a delicate balance of truth and lies that left no room for doubt. Jessica's family was convinced that she had finally found her happily ever after, and that I was just a distant memory, a mere footnote in the grand tome of her life.

But little did they know, I was just getting started. The disappearance of Jessica had been a mere appetiser, a taste of the darkness that lurked within me. And now, two years after, I had been ready to sink my teeth into my next victim.

It was during this time that I met Leah, a stunning nurse with piercing green eyes and raven-black hair. She was intelligent, witty, and had a spark in her eyes that seemed to ignite a fire within me. We met at the hospital where I had secured a placement, and from the moment we locked eyes, I knew she was the one to be next.

Leah was everything Jessica wasn't - confident, self-assured, and with a sharp tongue that could cut down even the most arrogant of individuals. But beneath her tough exterior, I sensed a vulnerability, a deep-seated insecurity that made her all the more appealing to me.

As we worked together on the ward, our conversations grew more frequent, more intimate. We would talk about everything and nothing, our words dancing around each other like lovers in the dark. And with each passing day, my obsession with Leah grew stronger.

I began to notice the way she moved with precision and purpose, her nurse's uniform clinging to her curves like a second skin. The way she smiled when she thought no one was looking, her eyes crinkling at the corners like delicate paper. And the way she laughed, oh god, the way she laughed - it was like music to my ears.

But Leah was different from Jessica in many ways. She was more cautious, more guarded. It would take time and effort to break down her defences, to peel away the layers of protection she had built around herself. And so, I bided my time, waiting for the perfect moment to strike.

Weeks turned into months, and our interactions became a frequent event. Each gesture, each word, was chosen with the precision of a master craftsman, designed to chip away at the fortress Leah had constructed around her heart, dark, like how I had become. Unlike Jessica, who opened like a blooming flower at the first touch of warmth, Leah required patience, an understanding that her walls weren't merely barriers but layers of experience in all ways.

Initially, our dates were public, boring but I don't care with yeah by my side. Coffee in bustling cafes, walks through local shopping centres, where the anonymity of the crowd allowed us to find safety. I listened, truly listened, to her stories, her laughter, her thoughts.

Then came the subtle shifts. Invitations to quieter areas, a secluded park bench under the watchful gaze of ancient trees, the soft rustle of leaves mirroring the quiet rhythm of her heart rate as she relaxed, just a fraction, in my presence. Conversations turned to our dark sides and one day upon getting our coffee things took a darker turn.

As I sat with Leah, sipping coffee and pretending to be a functioning member of society, she started to open up about her dark side. And by "dark side," I mean the kind of stuff that would make a serial killer raise an eyebrow. But hey, I'm all about exploring the depths of human depravity, so I leaned in and said, "tell me more, you delightful sociopath."

She started talking about her best friend, and how they had a... Let's call it a "complicated" relationship. Apparently, Leah had a fondness for forcing herself on her best friend when they were younger. Now, I know what you're thinking - "that's not funny, that's horrific!" and you're right, it is. But Leah told the story with such a nonchalant attitude, like she was talking about borrowing clothes without asking, that it was almost... Amusing? In a twisted way.

As she spoke, I could see the conflict within her - the guilt and shame warring with the thrill of getting away with something so heinous. It was like watching a train wreck in slow motion - you know it's going to end badly, but you can't look away.

I listened intently, trying not to laugh at the absurdity of it all. Not because I thought it was funny but because I wanted to understand what made Leah tick. What drives someone to do something so monstrous? Is it nature or nurture? Or is it just a case of being born without that whole "empathy" thing?

Anyway, as we chatted about rape and manipulation over coffee and croissants (because what's more civilised than discussing trauma over pastry?), I realised that Leah wasn't just some one-dimensional monster - she was complex and multifaceted (and also possibly insane). And honestly? That made her kind of fascinating.

As Leah continued to share her twisted tales, I found myself becoming increasingly enthralled. Her story about stealing medicine from the hospital and showing up to work high, only to have a patient die under her care whilst she watched, too high to care, now this should have been disturbing. But instead, I felt a thrill of excitement coursing through my veins.

There was something about Leah's nonchalant attitude, her cavalier disregard for human life, that drew me in. It was like she was speaking my language, and I was eager to respond. As she finished her story, I couldn't help but feel a sense of admiration for her audacity.

I leaned in closer, my eyes locking onto hers with an intensity that made her raise an eyebrow. "you know, Leah," I said, my voice low and husky, "I think it's time I shared a story of my own."

She smiled, a mischievous glint in her eye, and I knew she was intrigued. "oh?" she said, her voice barely above a whisper. "do tell."

I smiled back at her, feeling a sense of anticipation building inside me. "not here," I said, glancing around the crowded coffee shop. "but tonight... Under the moonlight... On the field next to the farm..."

Leah's eyes sparkled with understanding, and she nodded.. She knew what I was suggesting - not just that we would meet up later to share more stories but that we would take things further than that.

As we parted ways later that day after making plans for tonight, my mind began racing with thoughts. Jessica's face flashed before my eyes as anticipation grew. Tonight would be different though, it wouldn't be Jessica i'd be taking, but Leah - the girl who stole medicine from the hospital and showed no remorse had just become someone I really wanted to be my second girl.

As the sun dipped below the horizon, a beautiful orange glow filled the rolling hills and fields, I made my way to the designated meeting spot. The air was alive with the sweet scent of spring the, creating a sense of anticipation and excitement. I adjusted my worn-out jeans, which were clinging to my curves for dear life, and smoothed out my faded band t-shirt. My hair was a tangled mess, but I didn't care – I was too busy thinking about getting tangled up with Leah.

Leah was already there, her slender figure silhouetted against the moonlit sky. She turned to face me as I approached, a sly smile spreading across her lips. We didn't need to say a word; our eyes locked in a spark of mutual understanding.

Without hesitation, we walked towards each other, our bodies drawn together like magnets. The grass beneath our feet was soft and dewy, providing a natural cushion as we sank to the ground. Leah's hands were already working their way up my shirt, her fingers tracing intricate patterns on my skin.

I responded with my fingers dancing across her body, exploring every curve and contour. Her breasts were small but firm, fitting perfectly in the palm of my hand. I squeezed gently, feeling her nipples harden beneath my touch.

As we kissed, our tongues tangled together in a passionate dance. Leah's mouth was hot and hungry, devouring mine with an insatiable appetite. I felt myself getting lost in the sensation, my senses overwhelmed by the sheer intensity of our connection.

We broke apart for a moment, gasping for air as we gazed into each other's eyes. Leah's pupils were dilated, her irises gleaming with a feral light. I knew in that moment that she was mine for the taking.

"Hey," I said with a grin "you know what they say: 'the way to a woman's heart is through her stomach'... Or in this case... Through her vagina." Leah chuckled "well then let me be your chef tonight"

With that she slipped down between my legs spreading them wide open so she could see everything.

She leaned forward tongue darting in and out, that first lick sending shockwave coursing through every fibre of me. Each successive lick only intensified the sensations - a beautiful mix of pleasure pain of wanting more, I threw my head back, allowing myself to get completely lost.

As Leah's tongue continued to dance across my vulva, I felt the tension building up inside me. My hips began to buck, and my legs started to tremble. I was losing control, and it felt amazing.

Suddenly, I was hit with a wave of intense pleasure, and I let out a loud, animalistic scream. It was like nothing i'd ever experienced before. My body arched off the ground, and my hands grasped at the grass as if trying to ground myself to the earth.

Leah's mouth was still attached to me, drinking in every drop of my cum as I came hard into her mouth. The sensation was overwhelming, and I felt like I was going to pass out from sheer pleasure a feeling not many have given me, and definitely not like this.

As the last waves of my orgasm subsided, I turned to Leah with a mischievous grin spreading across my face. "it's your turn now," I said, my voice husky with desire.

Leah's eyes sparkled with anticipation as she nodded eagerly. But then I added a question that made her pause for a moment: "can I use Jessica?"

Leah raised an eyebrow " Jessica?" she repeated

I pulled out a my old gifted knife with its seductive red handle that seemed to glow better than before. "I've named her Jessica," I said with a chuckle "she's been with me for a while now."

Leah looked taken aback but also intrigued by the knife and its name.

"What do you plan on doing with... Jessica?" she asked hesitantly

I chuckled deep in throat "oh don't worry baby girl, i'll promise to be gentle...or not depending what you want"

Leah's eyes locked onto mine searchingly for moment then nodded almost imperceptibly.

With that I take out Jessica's blade -moonlight glinting off metal -and gently began trace patterns on

Leah's skin. The sensation sent shivers coursing through both our bodies...this night just got whole lot darker.

"we will use her later!" I smile. As I slipped my fingers into Leah's pussy, I couldn't help but think that this was the most fun i'd had all for a very long time.. Her folds were like a warm hug from the inside out, inviting me to explore every nook and cranny, and maybe even get lost in there forever. If only that was a possibility in this moment.

I began to finger her with a gentle touch, my fingertips pushing deep and fast onto her g-spot, sending shivers down her spine and making her eyes roll back in her head like as if possessed. Her warm juices started to flow, coating my fingers in a sticky film of desire, and I was pretty sure I heard the sound of my own personal demons cheering me on, clapping wildly.

As I pulled out, my thumb found its way to her clit, rubbing it with a soft circular motion that made her hips buckle and tremble like a wild bull. Leah's eyes locked onto mine, filled with a desperate longing for release, and I couldn't help but think that she had no idea what she was getting herself into.

I increased the pace of my fingering, my fingers curling and uncurling inside her like a tsunami destroying everything in its path. Leah's breathing grew fast, her chest heaving with anticipation, and I could practically hear the sound of her sanity slipping away.

And then, she came. Hard. Like "I-just-saw-god" hard. Her body convulsed around me, squeezing my fingers like a vice as she rode out the waves of pleasure. I felt like I was drowning in her ecstasy, swept away by the torrent of her release.

As she lay there panting and spent, I took out Jessica -my trusty blade- I gently pushed the crimson handle inside her still throbbing pussy. She let out low guttural moan,my hand moved up an down the handle -in an out- pretending Jessica was a cock that could make Leah cum all over again. Dirty talk spilled from lips "you love being fucked by Jessica, don't you"

But little did Leah know, Jessica had been used before...for much darker purposes...and now it I was using my own weird fantasy of Jessica fucking Leah. I know i'm fucked up but all the best people are, our brains are terrific things.

As I continued to move the handle in and out, Leah's moans grew louder, and her body began to tremble with another impending orgasm. I whispered more dirty talk into her ear, "you're going to come again, aren't you? You love being fucked by Jessica." finally, she let out a loud cry, and her body convulsed with pleasure.

Afterward, we lay there together, catching our breath. The moonlight streaming through the window above us cast an ethereal glow over the room. Leah turned to me, a curious glint in her eye. "you promised to tell me your dark secret," she reminded me, her voice barely above a whisper.

I laughed, a low, husky sound. "oh, it's nothing," I said, trying to brush it off. But Leah's eyes sparkled with intrigue, and she pressed me for more information. I sighed dramatically and said, "fine. If you must know... I killed my first love." I paused for effect before adding, "her name was Jessica."

Leah's expression changed from curiosity to skepticism. She raised an eyebrow and said, "you expect me to believe that? You're telling me that you killed someone named Jessica, and now you're using a blade with the same name to... Fuck me?" her voice trailed off as she searched my face for any sign of truth.

I just smiled and shrugged. "believe what you want," I said nonchalantly. But Leah wasn't buying it. She sat up and looked at me with a mixture of amusement and annoyance. "don't be ridiculous," she said. "you're not a killer. You're just trying to shock me or make yourself sound interesting." she shook her head and lay back down beside me. "try again," she whispered. "tell me something true."

I leaned in closer to Leah, my voice taking on a more serious tone. "I'm telling you, it's true," I said, my eyes locking onto hers. " Jessica was my first love, and I killed her. It was never meant to happen, but it happened nonetheless." I paused, studying Leah's reaction. She looked unsure, her expression a mix of fear and doubt.

"I was young and reckless," I continued, my words spilling out in a rush. "we were together, and things got out of hand. I didn't necessarily want to hurt her, but... It just happened." I shrugged.

Leah's face went pale, and she scrambled to sit up, putting distance between us. We were both lying naked there on a field of soft grass under the moonlight, a scene most would fantasise about but the fantasy had gone. Her eyes wide with fear as she stared at me like I was some sort monster that had been hiding beneath the surface all along

"you're... You're insane," she stuttered her voice trembling with each word. "how can you just casually talk about this?" she shook her head as if trying clear cobwebs from mind. "this isn't funny or interesting; it's twisted and sick."

Her voice rose to a loud shout as she pointed accusingly at me. "you're weird and twisted! How could you do something like that? And then use blade with her name to...to..." she trailed off unable to finish her sentence

I remained calm despite Leah growing hysterias my demeanour was almost aloof as she ranted because I was numb to Jessica now.

Leah jumped up from the grass we lay upon, backing away from me like I posed an immediate threat not knowing what I may do next. I mean I didn't plan too right now. The dew-kissed grass sparkled in the moonlight beneath our feet bar. Leah's feet moved swiftly as she moved farther away. Our naked bodies stood out starkly against the natural backdrop of the darkness.

"You need help" spat venomously.

As Leah turned ran away, I did have a second thought as to just let her go, but I couldn't. I wasn't ready to be caught, yet.

As I pursued Leah, my feet pounded against the dewy grass, and I rapidly closed the distance between us. It wasn't until I was mere steps behind her that I realised we were both still unclothed, our bodies exposed to the night air. The moonlight cast an ethereal glow over us, making our skin seem almost luminous as we ran.

I quickly gained on her and reached out to grab her arm, spinning her around to face me. She attempted to shake me off, but I held firm, my fingers digging into her skin as I pulled her back towards me. As she struggled against me, I wrapped my arms around her and took her down to the ground, pinning her beneath me.

"be quiet!" I shouted, my voice echoing through the night air as I tried to calm her down. "I would never harm you, Leah! You don't understand what's going on!" but Leah refused to be silenced. She continued to fight back with renewed ferocity, scratching at my face and kicking at my legs as she bucked beneath me.

Her eyes blazed with a fierce determination, and for a moment, I felt a surge of admiration for her spirit. However, as she continued to struggle and shout insults at me, my admiration quickly gave way to anger. Who did she think she was? Didn't she know that I had just shared something deeply personal with her? Didn't she care that I was trying to be honest with her?

My grip on her arms tightened as I leaned in closer, my face inches from hers. "stop it," I growled through gritted teeth. "just stop fighting and listen to me." but Leah refused to back down. She kept struggling and shouting until finally something inside of me snapped.

My anger boiled over like a pot left unattended on the stove, spilling out in a torrent of emotion. My vision narrowed, focusing solely on silencing this woman pinned beneath me who seemed so determined to spew venomous words. My mind clouded, reason lost amidst the swirling tempest of emotions raging free like an untamed beast unleashed upon the world.

In that moment, all rational thought abandoned me, leaving only primal instinct in its wake. The world around us melted away, leaving only the two of us locked in this desperate struggle. And as Leah continued to fight back, something dark within me began stirring - something ancient, primal, and altogether terrifying.

As the darkness within me grew, my grip on Leah's arms tightened, my fingers digging deeper into her skin. I could feel my anger and frustration boiling over, threatening to consume me whole. Leah's struggles grew more frantic, her eyes wide with fear as she realised the danger she was in.

My hands slid up her arms, my fingers wrapping around her throat like a vice. I could feel her pulse racing beneath my touch, and for a moment, I was tempted to squeeze tighter, to silence her once and for all. Leah's eyes went wide, her face turning red as she tried to struggle free.

But I held firm, my grip unyielding as I leaned in closer. "you shouldn't have come here," I whispered, my voice low and menacing. "you shouldn't have tried to leave." Leah's eyes were bulging now, her face purpling as she tried to gasp for air.

I could feel myself losing control, the darkness within me taking over. My vision narrowed to a single point - the woman struggling beneath me - and everything else faded away. The world around us melted into nothingness, leaving only the two of us locked in this desperate struggle.

And then, just as suddenly as it had begun, everything stopped. My hands relaxed their grip on Leah's throat, releasing their deadly pressure. She lay there, gasping for air, her chest heaving with exertion. For a moment, we just stared at each other, our eyes locked in a silent understanding.

The reality of what had almost happened hit me like a ton of bricks. I had almost killed her. The thought sent a shiver down my spine, and for a moment, I felt like I was staring into the abyss. But then something strange happened.

Leah looked up at me, and instead of fear or anger, I saw something else there - something that looked almost like curiosity. She reached out a trembling hand and touched my face, her fingers tracing the lines of my jaw. And then she spoke in barely above whisper "what made you this way ?".

As I sat there, staring at Leah's fragile form, I couldn't help but think of Jessica. She was the one who had set me on this path, who had unleashed the darkness within me. The memories of that night still lingered, the rush of adrenaline as I took her life, the thrill of power and control it gave me. For two years, I had craved that feeling again, but nothing seemed to satisfy me.

That was until I met Leah. There was something about her that sparked a fire within me, a flame that had been smouldering for so long. It started with a desire to possess her, to claim her as mine. But as I got to know her, I realised it was more than that. She brought out the anger and jealousy in me, the same emotions that had driven me to kill Jessica.

But tonight was different. Tonight, as I fucked her with a ferocity that bordered on violence, something unexpected happened. The adrenaline rush was there, but it wasn't enough to push me over the edge. For the first time in two years, I didn't want to kill.

Leah's reaction was puzzling. As she looked up at me with those curious eyes, I expected fear or revulsion. But instead, she seemed almost... Fascinated by me. Her touch on my face sent shivers down my spine, and for a moment, I felt like she saw beyond the monster that I had become.

She asked me what made me this way, and for a moment, I considered telling her. Telling her about Jessica, about the thrill of killing, about the emptiness that followed. But something held me back. Maybe it was fear of losing control, or maybe it was fear of being rejected.

Leah's eyes never left mine as she waited for an answer. Her chest still heaved with exertion, and her skin glistened with sweat. She looked vulnerable and strong at the same time, a combination that only added to my confusion.

As we sat there in silence, Leah reached out again and touched my face. This time, it wasn't just a gentle touch - it was an exploration. She traced my jawline, my lips, my eyes. And then she leaned in closer and kissed me.

The kiss sent shockwaves through my body. No one had kissed me like that before - not since Jessica. It wasn't just a kiss ; it was an acceptance. An acceptance of who I am - monster and all.

And in that moment, something shifted inside of me. Maybe it was hope.

As I sat there, wrapped in the aftermath of our intense encounter, I couldn't shake off the feeling that Leah was still a wild card. Her curiosity and fascination with me were intriguing, but they didn't necessarily mean she wouldn't report me to the authorities. I had, after all, just confessed to killing someone, and that was a secret that could land me in prison for life.

As I looked into her eyes, I saw a spark of excitement and intrigue, but I also saw a glimmer of uncertainty. She was drawn to me, but she was also scared. And scared people do unpredictable things. I knew that if she were to report me, it would be the end of everything. I wouldn't be able to talk my way out of it, not with the evidence she had witnessed firsthand.

I thought back to all the times I had been careful, all the times I had covered my tracks and made sure that no one suspected a thing. And now, with Leah knowing my darkest secret, I felt like I was teetering on the edge of disaster. One wrong move, one misplaced word, and it would all come crashing down.

I couldn't trust her, not yet. Maybe not ever. She was still an outsider, someone who didn't understand the depths of my darkness. And even if she thought she did, even if she thought she could handle it, I knew that she couldn't. No one could.

As we sat there in silence, her kiss still lingering on my lips, reality started creeping back. The adrenaline rush began wearing off. My mind went cold. Calculating.

Leah might have been curious, fascinated even, but at some point, her survival instincts would take over. At some point, fear would win out over fascination. When reality set back in for good - as inevitably as daybreak - then where would we be ? What then ?

And what about Jessica's blade ? What about our little game tonight ? All this evidence against me...

My grip around Leah tightened ever so slightly as these thoughts cascaded through my mind like ice water down a winter's night spine.

It wasn't personal anymore ; this had become purely transactional : how much longer until Leah cracks under pressure ?

As I held her close, my mind racing with the calculations, I could feel her warmth and vulnerability. It was a stark contrast to the icy grip of reality that was slowly suffocating me. I knew I had to keep her invested, keep her hooked on the thrill of being with me, no matter how fleeting it may be.

My eyes locked onto hers, searching for any sign of weakness, any crack in the facade. But all I saw was a spark of curiosity, a flame that flickered with excitement. It was intoxicating, and for a moment, I let myself get lost in its warmth.

But the chill of reality soon snapped me back to attention. I couldn't afford to get distracted, not now, not when the stakes were so high. The game with Jessica's blade still lingered, a constant reminder of the danger that lurked beneath the surface.

I leaned in closer to Leah, my voice taking on a low, husky tone. "you're playing with fire," I whispered, my breath dancing across her skin. "you know that, don't you?" my words were laced with warning, but also with temptation.

Leah's eyes never left mine, her gaze burning with an inner fire that seemed to match my own. For a moment, we just stared at each other, the air thick with tension.

And then she spoke up in barely above whisper "maybe I like playing games"

Her words hung in the air like a challenge, a gauntlet thrown down. Maybe she did like playing games, but I was the one who always came out on top. I was the one who held the power, who pulled the strings. And right now, I was holding her.

As I looked into her eyes, I saw a spark of defiance, of recklessness. It was a spark that I knew would eventually burn out, consumed by the crushing weight of reality. And when it did, she would be left with nothing but ashes and regret.

My grip around her tightened, my fingers digging deeper into her skin. She didn't flinch, didn't pull away. Instead, she leaned in closer, her lips brushing against mine.

It was a fatal mistake.

In that moment, I knew that she had to die. She was too much of a risk, too much of a liability. She had seen too much, knew too much. And soon enough, she would realise that she was in over her head.

I could feel my heart rate slowing down, my mind clearing of any doubts or hesitation. It was just business now, just a transaction to be completed.

I pulled back from her kiss and looked into her eyes once more time. My voice low "you should not have come here"

She raised an eyebrow "Oh, is this where you tell me I should not have accepted the dinner invitation ?"

A small smile crept onto my face "no, its where I tell you that you should not have tried to play with someone who has no intention of losing"

Leah's eyes widened slightly as realisation started creeping in. But it was already too late for regrets. My mind had been made up.

"You know, for someone so curious about darkness, you really don't understand it do you ?"

Leah swallowed hard "I...I think I do"

I chuckled low in my throat "Oh no, sweetheart. You don't understand anything. You see darkness as something exciting, something to be explored and discovered. But let me tell you something - darkness is not exciting. Its cold and calculating and ruthless"

My grip on her tightened further as I whispered "and i'm going to show you just how ruthless it can be

Leah's eyes were wide with fear now, but I just smiled at her "don't worry though - it will all be over soon"

As I held Jessica's blade in my hand, I could feel the adrenaline coursing through my veins like a potent elixir. It was a rush unlike any other, a high that only came from taking control, from exerting my dominance over the world. And Leah, with her naive curiosity and her reckless abandon, had just become my next fix.

I looked into her eyes, and for a moment, I saw a glimmer of understanding. She knew what was coming. She knew that she had pushed too far, that she had played with fire and gotten burned. And In that moment, I felt a twisted sense of excitement, a thrill that came from knowing I was about to unleash hell.

"Well, well, well," I said, my voice low and husky with anticipation. "looks like you should have stuck to playing with dolls instead of playing with fire." I chuckled to myself, the sound low and menacing. "but don't worry, i'll make sure your death is more exciting than your life ever was."

Then, with one swift motion, I slit her throat. The blade bit deep into her skin, and a crimson arc sprayed out from the wound like a fountain. Leah's eyes went wide with shock, and she tried to speak, but all that came out was a gurgling sound.

I held her close as she died, feeling her warm blood spill onto my skin like a dark baptism. It was almost... Intimate. A final embrace between us, a last moment of connection before she slipped away into nothingness.

As the life drained from her body, I couldn't help but feel invigorated. The rush of adrenaline was intoxicating, it made me feel alive. And as I stood there, holding her lifeless body in my arms, I couldn't help but think "you know what they say - all is fair in love and murder"

The darkness closed in around me, but I felt no fear. Only excitement. Only anticipation. Because I knew this was what I wanted, the adrenaline. There were more secrets to uncover, more lies to tell, more lives to take.

SEVEN

I was scrubbing out of a particularly gruelling surgery on which I was observing the terrific surgeons perform an appendectomy when I noticed a group of Leah's colleagues from the hospital huddled near the nurse's station. They were whispering among themselves, casting nervous glances in my direction.

As they approached me, I could sense a mix of concern and curiosity emanating from them. "Hey, have you seen Leah?" one of them asked, trying to sound casual.

I pulled off my gloves and leaned against the counter, adopting a thoughtful expression. "Actually, I did see her last week," I said, pausing for a moment to collect my thoughts. "We grabbed a cup of coffee together during our break and caught up on some old times."

The group exchanged skeptical glances, but I continued. "She mentioned that she was feeling really burned out from the long hours and high stress of working here. She said something about needing to take a little break and recharge her batteries."

One of her colleagues frowned. "But that's weird. She wouldn't just leave without telling us?"

I shrugged sympathetically. "I know it sounds strange, but she seemed really overwhelmed. She told me that she was thinking about taking some time off to visit her family in Spain and get some rest. Maybe she just needed some time to herself?"

The group nodded slowly, seeming to accept my explanation. One of them asked if I had heard from her since our coffee break, and I shook my head regretfully.

As they walked away, still looking concerned but slightly reassured, I felt a twinge of satisfaction. My story had been convincing enough to placate them for now.

Over the next few weeks, occasional questions about Leah's whereabouts would arise, each time I would spin another tale. Sometimes I would say I received a text from her saying how great it was to be spending time with family.

My goal was not only make everyone believe Leah left willingly but also distance myself as much as possible. Slowly people stopped asking questions, life moved forward as normal in the chaotic world of the hospital.

But deep down inside me - there will always be dark memories which only I knew. The smell of blood still lingered on my skin, reminders of the secrets I kept hidden behind my scrubs.

As the months slipped by, I found myself growing increasingly disconnected from the world around me. The hospital, which had once been a place of excitement and purpose, now felt suffocating, like a cage from which I couldn't escape. I couldn't shake the feeling that I was living a lie, that my secrets were slowly consuming me from the inside out. The memories of Leah and Jessica lingered like ghosts, haunting me relentlessly, their whispers echoing in the quiet corners of my mind. It felt like I was in a bad horror film, just waiting for the dramatic music to kick in.

I knew I had to get out, to escape the constant reminders of my past. So, I made the difficult decision to leave my placement at the hospital and attempt to start fresh. But fresh starts are hard to come by when you're burdened with the kind of emotional baggage I was carrying. It felt as though I was dragging an anchor behind me, weighing me down no matter how fast I tried to swim. Honestly, I was starting to feel like an overstuffed suitcase that just wouldn't close.

I drifted into retail work, taking on a series of unfulfilling jobs that allowed me to pay the bills but offered little in terms of emotional engagement. Each day blended into the next, a monotonous cycle of folding clothes and ringing up purchases. It was a hollow existence, but it provided me with the freedom to pursue my true passions: writing and indulging in my darker fascinations. Who knew that folding t-shirts could become a gateway to penning my next gothic novel?

In the solitude of my parents' house, which they had left to me and my brother, I spent hours scribbling away in battered notebooks, pouring out my thoughts and fantasies onto the page. I wrote about death and destruction, about bloodlust and chaos. Each word was a cathartic release, yet it only seemed to fuel my desires for more—a twisted kind of hunger that gnawed at me relentlessly. I often looked at the old post it notes surrounding the room.

When I wasn't working or writing, I tried to fill the void with fleeting connections with others. I would pick up men and women in bars or clubs, seeking out those brief, adrenaline-fuelled moments of intimacy that would distract me from the emptiness inside. I knew I preferred a woman's body but the penetration of a man sometimes filled something that was missing. But no matter how thrilling those encounters were, they were never enough. The highs were temporary, and soon i'd find myself crashing back down into the darkness that loomed just beneath the surface. It was like a rollercoaster ride where the only thing waiting for you at the end was a sad, empty cotton candy stick.

My social life was sparse and superficial, a series of faces that came and went without ever truly getting close. No one could see behind the carefully constructed mask I wore, except for Joey. He was different somehow—perhaps it was because he knew nothing about my troubled past or that he thought my obsession with horror writing was just a quirky hobby.

Joey would come over to our family's old farmhouse, where I lived with my brother. We'd spend hours talking and watching movies together, enveloped in a comfortable camaraderie that felt like a lifeline amidst the chaos. The farmhouse, once a vibrant hub of family activity, now lay in disarray. My parents' legacy was slowly decaying around us, largely due to my brother's complete disinterest in maintaining anything—especially not the farm-related chores that had fallen squarely on my shoulders since childhood. Seriously, if the house had a voice, it would probably be begging for a good housekeeping award, I can hear how angry my mother would have been.

Despite the neglect that surrounded us, Joey remained a genuinely attentive and caring individual. He didn't pry into my hidden secrets; instead, he offered a kindness that was both refreshing and comforting. He was always mindful, polite, and considerate—a beacon of light during an otherwise dark, endless nightmarish rollercoaster ride that played out in vivid, macabre imagery within my mind, 24/7. I sometimes wondered if he was secretly a therapist in disguise, but thankfully, he never charged me by the hour.

Joey was the kind of guy who had an easy charm that could turn a frown upside down faster than you could say "awkward small talk." with tousled brown hair that looked like it had been styled by a particularly enthusiastic squirrel and a smile that could light up even the dullest of days, he had an infectious energy that drew people in. He was tall and lean, with a laid-back vibe that suggested he'd just rolled out of bed—though I suspected he had a secret stash of hair gel hidden somewhere.

I first met Joey at the local library, the very place I used to loathe Jessica for frequenting. Libraries were supposed to be hallowed halls of knowledge, not the backdrop for my most intense eye-rolling sessions. But there I was, trying to avoid the overwhelming nostalgia of my past and the ghosts of memories that lingered in the aisles. As I was attempting to find a distraction in a dusty horror novel, I heard a voice behind me. "excuse me, do you have a map? Because I keep getting lost in those shelves."

I turned around to see Joey, looking like he'd just stepped out of a music video, grinning like he'd just told the best joke in the world. He was hunting for the non-fiction section, but clearly he had no idea where he was going. I couldn't help but laugh at his absurdity. "you're in the wrong section, my friend. This is where we keep the scary stories, not the self-help books."

Despite his attractiveness, there was something about Joey that made it clear we were worlds apart when it came to intimacy. He was like a brother to me, a confidant who provided comfort and companionship without any romantic undertones. We began to meet regularly, often devolving into debates over whether horror movies were better with or without jump scares (he was a staunch advocate for the latter, claiming that the only thing scarier than a ghost popping out was the prospect of a bad date).

Joey had a way of listening that made you feel heard, truly heard, rather than just waiting for his turn to speak. Whenever I vented about my life, he'd nod thoughtfully, occasionally throwing in a quip that felt like a warm hug wrapped in a punchline. "you know," he'd say, "if your life were a sitcom, it'd definitely be a dark comedy. Just add a laugh track, and we're golden."

Yet, despite his charms and the undeniable chemistry between us, the thought of anything romantic with Joey felt as foreign as trying to read Shakespeare in

Klingon. I couldn't imagine crossing that line; it would be like trying to turn a comfy pair of sweatpants into a tuxedo–pointless and a bit ridiculous. Our friendship was a sanctuary, a rare and precious bond free from the complexities of romance.

In a way, I was grateful for this dynamic. It allowed us to navigate the shadows together without the added pressure of romantic entanglements. I found comfort in our platonic friendship, knowing that with Joey, I could just be myself–no masks, no pretences. He was my anchor in a turbulent sea, and I wouldn't trade that for anything.

As time went on, my friendship with Joey blossomed into a comfortable routine of laughter and camaraderie. We spent countless hours together, navigating the ups and downs of life with our usual blend of humour and sarcasm. However, things took a rather unfortunate turn when Joey met Larissa.

It all started innocently enough–one fateful day at the library, Joey casually mentioned that he had met someone. I was excited for him; after all, he deserved to find love. But when he said her name, it felt like a dark cloud rolled in over our sunshine-filled conversations. Larissa. Just saying her name made my skin crawl, like stepping on a slug in the dark.

Larissa was the kind of woman who could stop traffic with a single glance. She was way too hot–like, "did she just walk off the cover of a magazine?" Hot. With long, flowing hair that looked like it belonged in a shampoo commercial and legs for days, she had this air of confidence that made you wonder if she had a secret deal with the universe. I swear, when she walked into a room, even the lights seemed to dim in comparison. I had the misfortune of meeting her at a small gathering Joey hosted to introduce us. I remember walking into the room and immediately feeling the urge to flee.

"Hi! I'm Larissa," she chirped, her voice as sweet as a sugar-coated razor blade. She immediately launched into a monologue about her latest yoga retreat—complete with instagram photos that felt less like sharing and more like a parade of self-indulgence. I stood there, trying to muster a polite smile while my inner monologue screamed, "what is she even talking about?!"

Joey, of course, was smitten. I watched in dismay as he hung on her every word, oblivious to the eye rolls and side glances exchanged among our friends. I couldn't understand what he saw in her—she was like a walking Pinterest board gone rogue, and I was convinced she was using some sort of mind control on him.

The more time they spent together, the more I found myself dreading our hangouts. Larissa would often tag along, and I felt like I was trapped in a never-ending episode of a reality show that I didn't want to be a part of. Every time Joey and I would try to share a laugh or a moment, she'd swoop in with her unsolicited opinions, turning the conversation into a one-woman show. "oh, you two are so cute together!" She'd coo, completely missing the point that we were just friends.

It became a running joke between my other mates and me. "What's the latest Larissa update?" They'd ask, barely able to contain their laughter. I couldn't help but roll my eyes. "oh, you know, she's probably off saving the world one overpriced smoothie at a time," i'd reply with a dramatic sigh.

Despite my growing disdain for her, I tried to be supportive of Joey. I wanted him to be happy, but it was hard to watch him fall deeper for someone who seemed to live in a bubble of self-importance. I often found myself plotting elaborate scenarios in my head where Larissa would trip over her own ego and take a long holiday away from us—preferably somewhere really remote, like a deserted island with no wi-fi.

"Maybe she'll get lost in a corn maze," I joked to Joey one evening when I couldn't hold back any longer. "or better yet, maybe she'll find herself on a reality show and never come back!"

Joey just laughed, blissfully unaware of the storm brewing in my heart. "you're being dramatic," he said, shaking his head. "she's really great once you get to know her."

I wanted to scream, "No! She's not! She's a human black hole of personality!" But instead, I bit my tongue, forcing a smile that probably looked more like a grimace. I reminded myself of the importance of friendship and how I didn't want to sabotage Joey's happiness, even if it meant enduring Larissa's presence.

As their relationship progressed, I found myself torn between being a supportive friend and wanting to stage an intervention. I could only hope that someday, Joey would see Larissa for who she truly was—an overhyped, self-absorbed goddess who had somehow bewitched him. Until then, I would have to endure this new chapter with a sense of humour, hoping my eye rolls wouldn't become permanent fixtures on my face. After all, if I survived Jessica, I could survive anything—even Larissa.

As Joey and Larissa's relationship blossomed, I found myself in an increasingly absurd situation. It was like being stuck in a sitcom where the laugh track never stopped, but the jokes were all terrible. Larissa's presence turned our hangouts into a bizarre game of verbal dodgeball, where I was always on the receiving end of her passive-aggressive barbs.

"Hey, there you are!" Larissa would say with a saccharine smile that made my teeth ache. "I didn't know you were still hanging around, trying to be Joey's 'cool' friend." The way she said "cool" made it sound like she was describing a particularly unpleasant smell.

I'd plaster on my best fake smile and respond, "well, you know me—just here to keep the fun alive. Someone has to make sure Joey doesn't turn into a yoga mat or something."

Her eyes would narrow slightly, and I could almost hear the gears turning in her head as she plotted her next zinger. "oh, I wouldn't worry about that! He's too busy learning about the benefits of kale smoothies to think about anything so mundane."

It was as if she took joy in reminding me that I was a mere sidekick in this bizarre rom-com of their lives. She had this uncanny ability to twist every conversation to her advantage, turning the focus back to her latest "adventures" as if the world was just waiting with bated breath for her updates.

One evening, we were all sat together at a pub—Joey, Larissa, and me, awkwardly crammed into a booth that felt more like a confessional than a casual hangout. Joey ordered a round of drinks, and I seized the opportunity to try and connect with Larissa, hoping to find some common ground.

"So, Larissa, what do you do for fun when you're not being fabulous?" I asked, trying to sound genuinely interested.

"Oh, you know, just the usual!" She chirped, tossing her hair over her shoulder. "I go to exclusive art galleries, volunteer at charity galas, and try to save the planet one eco-friendly product at a time. What about you? Still writing your little horror stories?"

I could practically feel the eye roll forming before I even responded. "You could say that. I'm working on a new one about a woman who uses her looks to manipulate everyone around her. It's a real thriller!" I shot a glance at Joey, who was blissfully unaware of the tension building.

Larissa's smile faltered for just a moment, but she quickly recovered, her voice dripping with condescension. "Oh, how charming. I'm sure it'll be a bestseller—right next to those 'I survived my roommate' memoirs."

I could feel the heat rising in my cheeks, but I kept my cool. "yeah, well, at least my stories don't involve a Pinterest board for every meal I eat."

Joey, sensing the awkwardness, tried to change the subject. "so, Larissa, how's your new fitness regimen going?"

"Oh, it's incredible!" She beamed, completely ignoring my jab. "i'm training for a marathon, and i've never felt better. I just love pushing my limits!"

"Right," I muttered under my breath, "Because running away from personality is a sport now."

Larissa shot me a look that could've frozen lava. "You know, not everyone can appreciate the finer things in life, like health and fitness. Some people are just... comfortable being mediocre."

I couldn't help but laugh—partly out of disbelief and partly because, let's face it, her words were so over-the-top they could have been a parody. "oh, please! I'm just trying to keep my standards low, so I can relate to others on my level."

The tension was thick enough to cut with a knife, and Joey looked back and forth between us, his eyes wide with confusion. "guys, let's just have a good time," he said, probably wishing he could summon a time machine to erase the last five minutes.

Despite the verbal sparring, I found amusement in the ridiculousness of it all. Every encounter felt like an episode of a sitcom gone awry, and I was the reluctant cast member desperately trying to avoid the spotlight. I could see Larissa for what she was—a self-absorbed diva who thrived on attention. But the more she tried to get under my skin, the more I was determined to keep my sense of humour intact.

As their relationship continued, I resigned myself to the fact that i'd have to endure Larissa's presence. I often joked with my work colleagues that I was writing a new story titled "the adventures of Joey, Larissa, and the friend who just can't even." Little did I know, the plot twists were far from over.

As the days turned into weeks, my frustration with Larissa evolved into a full-blown rage that simmered just beneath the surface. Each time I saw Joey and Larissa together, it felt like adding another log to a fire that was already roaring out of control. It was like watching a slow-motion train wreck, and I was stuck on the platform, unable to look away.

Larissa had this remarkable talent for making every situation about her. One afternoon, we all went out for lunch, and I made the mistake of ordering a salad. "oh, wow, how original," she said, her perfectly manicured eyebrows arching in feigned disbelief. "I thought you'd go for something more exciting, like… I don't know, a fancy avocado toast. You know, something trendy."

I could feel my blood pressure rising. "well, i'm just trying to avoid an avocado toast-induced existential crisis, thank you very much."

Joey laughed, blissfully unaware of the tension brewing. "c'mon, you both should give it a try! It's surprisingly good."

Larissa jumped in, "oh, I can only imagine how hard it is to eat a salad when you could be enjoying the culinary delight of instagram-able food! But then again, some people wouldn't know the difference." A thinly veiled jab, and I was starting to wonder if she had a secret handbook on how to annoy me.

Every time we hung out, it felt like I was in a competition I never signed up for. Larissa would casually mention her "influencer" friends or the latest exclusive event she attended, throwing in phrases like "you wouldn't know them" as if they were the names of ancient philosophers. I felt like I was in a reality show where the prize was to endure her relentless need for validation.

One evening, Joey invited me over for movie night. "just the three of us!" He said, excitement radiating from him. I should have known better. When I arrived, Larissa was already there, decked out in a form-fitting outfit that could only be described as "i'm here to steal your thunder." She had already set up an elaborate spread of popcorn, candy, and—of course—gluten-free snacks that looked suspiciously like cardboard.

"Are you ready for a proper horror movie?" I asked, trying to sound enthusiastic.

"Oh, sweetie," she replied, her voice dripping with condescension, "I only watch films that are critically acclaimed. I mean, I can't waste my time on something that doesn't have at least an 80% rating on rotten tomatoes."

"Right, because watching a movie about a killer cornfield is clearly beneath you," I shot back, trying to hold on to my sanity.

"Exactly!" She beamed, completely missing the sarcasm. "you get it!"

With each interaction, I felt a little piece of my soul getting chipped away, like I was slowly being worn down by the relentless tide of her superiority complex. She had this knack for turning every conversation into a competition, making me question my worth as a friend. I often found myself biting my tongue, desperate not to lash out and ruin joey's good mood.

But the final straw came during a dinner party at Joey's place. I had been looking forward to it, hoping it would be a lovely evening filled with laughter and banter. Instead, Larissa took it upon herself to turn the gathering into a showcase of her own accomplishments. "did I tell you about the time I was featured in a lifestyle magazine?" She asked, her eyes sparkling with delight. "they called me a 'rising star in the wellness community!'"

I choked on my drink, trying not to laugh. "well, it sounds like you're doing better than most of us mere mortals!"

"Oh, darling, it's not about doing better—it's about elevating the whole experience." She smiled as if she'd just delivered the world's most profound nugget of wisdom.

I could feel the heat rising in my cheeks as I glanced at Joey, who was watching her with a silly grin. "That's amazing, Larissa!" He gushed, clearly enamoured..

"Yeah, amazing," I muttered under my breath. "if only the universe would stop revolving around you for a second."

As the evening progressed, I could feel my anger bubbling over. Every time she spoke, it was like nails on a chalkboard, and I was on the verge of a meltdown. I could practically hear the universe snickering at my predicament.

When the night finally came to an end, and I left joey's flat, I felt a mix of frustration and hilarity at the absurdity of it all. It was like living in a bizarre sitcom where I was the only character not in on the joke. I resolved that I needed to find a way to cope with Larissa or risk turning into a full-fledged cartoon villain, complete with a maniacal laugh and a sinister plot to send her packing.

Joey

EIGHT

As the days turned into a blur of Larissa's relentless cheerfulness, I felt my sanity teetering on the edge of a cliff. Each time she laughed or fluttered her eyelashes at Joey, it was like watching a cat play with a mouse. And I was the mouse—exhausted, cornered, and ready to snap.

The plan began innocently enough. I found myself sketching out scenarios in my notebook, each one more outrageous and darkly humorous than the last. "operation eliminate Larissa" became my secret project, a twisted blend of gallows humour and creative expression.

As I daydreamed about my increasingly ludicrous scenarios, a dark chuckle escaped my lips. "ah, sweet Larissa," I mused, "you have no idea the monsters I have unleashed in me."

The weight of what i'd done in the past, and what I was planning, was starting to feel less like a thrill and more like a persistent, unwelcome companion. I was used to the darkness now, it was a part of me. But the idea of it always being with me was beginning to be less like my familiar and more like a roommate who refuses to pay rent. Still, I was committed to the hunt. And Larissa, oh sweet, over-sugared Larissa, was still very much in my sights.

I had to admit, the initial thrill of the chase had morphed into something... exasperating. She was like a golden retriever that had decided to become a social media influencer: relentlessly enthusiastic, prone to dramatic pronouncements about organic kale smoothies, and utterly oblivious to the chaos she left in her wake.

But her relentless facade also intrigued me. Was it a mask? A coping mechanism? Or was she truly that... shallow? I decided to dig deeper, and my plan to "deal with her" shifted from straight up death to slow burn murder, I wanted to torment.

One evening, Joey, bless his oblivious heart, dragged me to a bar in the next town. "you two need to hang out," he'd said, oblivious to the fact that "hanging out" with Larissa felt like wading through a swamp of forced positivity. "get to know each other better! Bond over, you know, things."

And there she was, looking like she'd just stepped out of a yoga magazine – impossibly tan, with an outfit that probably cost more than my entire wardrobe. She had a gaggle of friends with her, a squad i'd affectionately nicknamed "the glitterati." they were, as I quickly discovered, the polar opposite of Larissa: refreshingly down-to-earth and possessed of a wit that made the evening almost bearable.

"Dahlia, darling!" Larissa chirped, grabbing me in a bone-crushing hug. "so glad you could make it! We're having a pre-concert party for... well, you wouldn't know them. They're quite underground." (the band turned out to be some derivative pop group that sounded like every other band.)

Her friends, however, were a different story. There was Maya, a fiery redhead with a razor-sharp tongue and a penchant for vintage clothing. Then there was Chloe, a sardonic artist who spent the entire evening sketching caricatures of people. Finally, there was sam, a quiet, thoughtful musician with a dry wit that could leave you in stitches.

"Don't mind her," Maya said, rolling her eyes as Larissa preened in the corner. "she thinks she's the main character of a bad romantic comedy."

"Oh, you have no idea," I muttered, grinning back at Maya.

As the night wore on, I found myself drawn to Larissa's friends. They were clever, observant, and unafraid to poke fun at their friend's more... flamboyant tendencies. They also seemed genuinely interested in getting to know me, asking about my writing and my life, as if I wasn't a psycho.

"So," Chloe said, sketching in her notebook, "what kind of twisted horrors do you conjure up for your little stories, Dahlia?"

"Oh, the usual," I said, a smile playing on my lips. "obsession, manipulation, and the occasional surprise dismemberment."

Sam let out a low whistle. "sounds intense. And yet, somehow, you seem… normal?"

"I have my moments," I replied, glancing at Larissa, who was now trying to convince a bouncer to let her backstage. "I just keep them to myself."

Maya raised her glass. "to dark stories, and friends who keep you grounded in reality. Or at least, try to."

We all clinked glasses, leaving Larissa to her own devices. For a brief, shining moment, I felt a connection. Maybe it was the shared laughter, the easy conversation, or the sense of genuine acceptance. Whatever it was, it was intoxicating, and I felt a tinge of regret that this night would inevitably end.

Larissa eventually returned, looking slightly deflated. The bouncer, apparently, was not impressed by her instagram followers. "they wouldn't even let me in!" she whined. "they said I wasn't on the list!"

"Oh, the humanity," sam deadpanned, earning a sharp glare from Larissa.

The rest of the night was a blur of bad music, overpriced drinks, and increasingly awkward small talk. Larissa managed to turn every conversation back to herself, and I found myself increasingly annoyed by her self-absorption.

As we finally left the bar, stumbling out into the cool night air, I couldn't help but think about the contrast between Larissa and her friends. They were real, they were relatable, and, most importantly, they weren't constantly trying to sell you something.

"Well," I said to Joey and Larissa as we waited for a taxi, "that was… an experience."

"Tell me about it," Maya said, appearing beside us. "come on, let's go do something fun."

Larissa turned to me, her smile as bright as a faulty headlight. "You know, Dahlia, I'm starting to think we could be real friends."

"Oh, I'm sure you'll try to manipulate me," I said, hoping to at least put a slight chink in her armour. "but I have a feeling that it won't be as easy as it was with Jessica." I had to make her understand I was in control, just like with Jessica.

Larissa froze, and for a moment, I thought I saw a flicker of fear in her eyes. But it was gone in an instant, replaced by her usual facade of confidence.

"Don't be ridiculous!" she scoffed. "we all have secrets, darling. I'm a firm believer in embracing them all."

As I watched her preen and pose for a selfie, I realised that the thrill of the chase had been replaced by something more complicated: a dark, twisted game of cat and mouse, where the rules were constantly changing.

This was definitely not what I had intended. It was no longer about killing, it was about the challenge and the fun. And in that moment, I felt myself getting excited about what would happen next.

And there it was, my dark obsession. It's going to be a long journey.

The taxi ride back was a cacophony of drunken noise. Larissa, fuelled by something that resembled champagne mixed with pure, unadulterated ego, was attempting to sing along to the radio, badly. Joey was, predictably, too drunk to notice, and I, armed with a healthy dose of Jim Beam and Coke, was in the delicate balance between observing the chaos and enjoying the show.

"You know," Larissa slurred, leaning heavily into me, "I think... I think we should all go back to the flat. We can keep the party goin'! Joey, you agree?"

Joey, who had been attempting to re-tie his shoelaces for the past ten minutes, looked up with a glazed expression. "back? To the... flat? Sounds... groovy."

I, of course, agreed immediately. It wasn't just the adrenaline I was after anymore. I was starting to find this whole dynamic... fascinating. Larissa's desperate need for attention, Joey's cluelessness, and the potential for the unpredictable was a tempting concoction, all things considered. Plus, the thought of seeing how far I could push things was starting to tickle me.

We stumbled into their meticulously decorated flat – all minimalist furniture and aggressively neutral colours – and the party immediately took a turn for the worse. Or perhaps, better, depending on your perspective.

Larissa, convinced that she was a world-class mixologist, started concocting increasingly questionable cocktails. Joey, now fully horizontal on the couch, started rambling about his ex-girlfriend and how she "just didn't understand him." I, for my part, kept the Jim Beam flowing, watching it all unfold with a detached amusement.

The night went on, the alcohol took its toll. At some point, the conversation drifted into dangerous territory.

"You know, Dahlia," Larissa said, slurring her words as she stumbled towards me, a dangerous glint in her eye. "you're… you're kind of hot."

"Oh, really?" I replied, feigning surprise, secretly pleased with the way things were progressing.

"Yeah!" she continued. "and Joey… Well, he's… you know."

Joey, who was now snoring softly, offered no immediate protest.

I leaned in close to Larissa, close enough that I could smell the sweet, cloying scent of her perfume and the sour tang of the cheap liquor on her breath. "and what do you suggest, darling?"

She giggled, a high-pitched, almost manic sound. "Maybe… maybe we could all, you know…"

"Maybe," I finished for her, a slow smile spreading across my face. This was it.

The moment hung in the air, thick with unspoken desires and reckless abandon. I felt my pulse quicken, my senses sharpen. The thrill of the unknown, the rush of danger, and the sheer absurdity of the situation were all in motion.

I was prepared for her to start things immediately, after all, her intentions were clear. I had the adrenaline pumping, the control, the situation. I was going to enjoy this.

But then, to my surprise, Larissa started to cry. Great big, heaving sobs that shook her entire body.

"I... I don't know what I want!" she wailed, burying her face in her hands. "I'm such a mess. Everything's a mess."

Joey, jolted awake by the noise, sat up and blinked around at the scene. " Larissa? Honey? You okay?"

"No!" she sobbed. "I'm not okay! I'm completely and utterly not okay!"

She looked at me, her mascara running down her face, and I could see, for the first time, a flicker of real vulnerability in her eyes. This was the mask cracking, just a tiny bit, and it was, dare I say it, more compelling than all her preening and posturing. I was actually enjoying this.

Joey, bless his heart, tried to comfort her, wrapping his arms around her and whispering soothing words. "it's okay, baby. Everything's gonna be okay."

I watched them, a strange feeling, like a mixture of pity and frustration, washing over me. This wasn't how it was supposed to go. The dark, violent thoughts I had been having were no longer at the forefront of my mind.

"I think," I said, standing up, "that I should probably go. You guys need to sort this out."

Larissa looked up at me, her eyes red and swollen. "Don't go, Dahlia," she pleaded. "please… stay."

I hesitated. I wanted to walk away, to leave this mess of emotions and broken expectations behind. But there was also a part of me that was intrigued, that wanted to see where this unexpected turn would take us.

The adrenaline was still coursing through me. The excitement had merely shifted. The hunt had changed. And I knew, with a growing sense of dread and anticipation, that I wasn't going anywhere.

I sat back down on the couch, taking another swig of my drink. "Fine," I said. "but I'm staying out of it."

"You promise?" Larissa asked, her voice trembling.

"I promise," I said, and I found myself meaning it.

Okay, let's go there. Buckle up.

The next thing I knew, the harsh glare of morning sunlight was slicing through the blinds, assaulting my throbbing head. I was sprawled on the couch, a blanket haphazardly thrown over me. The remnants of the party were everywhere: empty bottles, half-filled glasses, a lingering smell of stale alcohol and cheap perfume.

I sat up, immediately regretting it. The world swam into a hazy, nauseating blur. As my vision cleared, I noticed two things: first, the lingering ache of Jim Beam coursing through my veins, and second, the sound of gentle snores coming from the floor beside me.

I looked down. Joey was lying there, completely naked, his face buried in a pillow. And, intertwined with him, her head resting on his chest, was Larissa. Also naked.

My brain stuttered. My carefully constructed plans – the meticulously crafted scenarios of manipulation and control – seemed to evaporate in the harsh light of day. I felt a surge of something akin to… bewilderment? Amusement? Disappointment? It was a confusing cocktail of emotions.

Larissa stirred, her eyes fluttering open. She blinked, then her gaze locked onto mine. Her expression shifted from sleep-dazed confusion to a slow dawning horror.

"Oh. My. God," she breathed, her voice barely a whisper. "what… what happened?"

She sat up, pulling the blanket around herself. Joey, oblivious to the drama unfolding, continued to snore.

I shrugged. "Looks like you and Joey had a good night."

Her face was a mask of confusion. "But… I… I don't remember…"

"Shocking," I deadpanned, taking a swig of my own, already prepared, bottled water.

She stared at me, then at Joey, then back at me again. Her face contorted in a mixture of shame and disbelief.

"I… I don't understand," she stammered. "I don't…"

"It's simple," I said, relishing the moment. "you got drunk. You ended up in bed with your boyfriend. And here we all are."

She turned, her face ashen. She nudged Joey and whispered in his ear, "Joey, wake up!"

Joey grunted, then slowly opened his eyes. He looked around, confused, then his gaze landed on Larissa, next to him. He looked at her naked, then at me. A slow grin spread across his face.

"Hey, good morning, Dahlia," he said. "Did we… did we have a good night?"

Larissa glared at him. "Joey!"

He looked from her to me, the grin fading. The colour drained from his face. He was completely mortified.

"Oh, crap," he mumbled. "oh, crap, crap, crap."

Larissa scrambled away from him, mortified, clutching the blanket to her chest. She was actually mortified, I had to smile.

"I… I need to get dressed," she said, her voice trembling. "I have to go."

She stumbled to her feet, almost tripping over a stray shoe. Without a word to either of us, she practically fled the room.

Joey remained frozen, staring at the space where she had been. The realisation of what had happened – the public display of his lack of prowess, the possibility of... betrayal? – was slowly sinking in.

He looked at me, his eyes wide with a mixture of panic and confusion. "Dahlia... what... what do I do?"

I leaned back on the couch, watching the morning drama unfold before me. I knew that he did not know that this was the plan, I almost felt bad. Almost.

"Well," I said, suppressing a laugh. "that depends. Do you want to chase after her, or do you want to sit here and contemplate the mysteries of human behaviour? Your choice."

He looked at me, bewildered. "But... but what happened? Why...?"

I shrugged. "You were drunk. She was drunk. Life is messy."

He took a deep breath, then slowly stood up. He was still naked, I had to laugh.

"I... I need to talk to her," he said, his voice wavering. "I have to fix this."

He hesitated for a moment, then turned and headed out the door after Larissa.

I was left alone in the wreckage, the aftermath of a night I hadn't even orchestrated. I was also left with a strange sensation. It was a mix of amusement, frustration, and a touch of... something akin to disappointment? This wasn't how I had planned for the night to go at all. I mean, it did, but the actual doing part was out of the question.

Okay, let's see where this messy aftermath takes us. We have Joey chasing after Larissa, a lot of raw emotion in the air, and me, sitting in the middle of the mess. Here's where I think we could go:

I watched the door swing shut behind Joey, the slam echoing in the suddenly silent flat. I took another long swig of water, letting it soothe my head, then slowly surveyed the scene. It was a disaster. A glorious, chaotic disaster.

A plan began to form in my mind. The old, predictable one was gone, now replaced by a new, more tantalising, and definitely darker one.

I got to my feet and began gathering up the debris. The remnants of the night, a broken string of pearls, a scattered magazine, a lost earring. I had to decide if I should leave, or stay and cause some more damage.

I walked over to the mirror in the hallway. My reflection was a mess, my clothes rumpled, my makeup smeared. But my eyes, they held a spark. I saw the glimmer of a new game.

I heard the lock on the front door click again. Joey stumbled back in, his face a mask of anguish.

"She's... she's gone," he said, his voice choked. "she said... she said she needs time."

He looked at me, his eyes pleading. "what am I supposed to do, Dahlia? What did I do wrong?"

I shrugged, feigning nonchalance. "maybe you weren't exciting enough."

His jaw dropped. He looked at me, genuinely shocked. "That's… that's not fair!"

"Life isn't fair, darling," I said, a smirk playing at the corner of my lips. "you really want her back? You want to salvage this… relationship? You're going to need to be less boring."

I knew, deep down, that this wasn't just about a broken relationship. It was about something deeper, something more fundamental. A hunger for control. I wanted to watch them unravel.

"What do you mean?" he asked, confused.

"Let me explain" I said as I walked towards him.

I leaned in close to Joey, close enough that he could smell my scent and the cheap liquor that still lingered on my breath.

"You need to show her that you can be unpredictable, exciting. Show her that there are things she doesn't know about you."

I moved closer and whispered in his ear "I know what she wants".

He flinched, his eyes widening.

"Show her you have another side. The darker side. The one that takes risks."

I paused, letting the silence stretch, letting my words sink in.

"If she doesn't like it, maybe you don't want her."

I pulled back, and smiled. "She doesn't know what she wants. You can show her".

The spark of a wicked idea began to burn in my mind. I was going to play this game with Joey, and play it well.

"Dahlia," Joey said, his eyes glinting with something other than the usual mischief. "we need to talk."

My heart skipped a beat. Joey had never been one for serious conversations, especially not with that tone. We sat down in the living room, the setting sun casting long shadows across the floor. The smell of dinner that i'd put on for us both wafted in from the kitchen, a comforting scent that seemed to relieve the tension in the air.

I studied him as he searched for the right words, his fingers drumming an erratic rhythm on his knee. He looked so nervous, so unlike the confident man who had swept me off my feet as a good friend years ago. His broad shoulders tensed under his t-shirt, and I couldn't help but let my gaze linger on the way his muscles moved beneath the fabric.

Finally, he took a deep breath. "Dahlia," he started again, "I don't know how to say this, but... I need to tell you something."

The silence stretched out like a tightrope between us. The only sound was the faint ticking of the clock on the wall, echoing in the quiet room. I felt like I was holding my breath, waiting for him to continue, but the words just weren't coming.

"It's about us," he said, his voice barely above a murmur. "I think... We need to try something new."

My mind raced, trying to anticipate what he might be about to suggest. New? What could be new? I friend zoned him ages who's but Joey had a knack for surprises, and I found myself both anxious and excited for what he had in mind.

"What do you mean?" I asked, my voice as soft as the fabric of the couch beneath me.

He looked at me, his eyes dark with passion and something else - something I couldn't quite put my finger on. "I want to... Take things to the next level."

I swallowed hard, feeling a thrill of excitement mingle with a hint of fear. The way he was looking at me, like he was ready to devour me whole, was making it hard to focus on anything but the desire pooling in my stomach.

"What kind of level?" I managed to get out.

He leaned in, his breath hot against my ear. "The kind of level that involves you, me, and no inhibitions."

I could feel his cock hardening against my thigh, and my own body responded in kind. It was like a dance we had never performed before.

"Are you sure?" I whispered, my hand instinctively moving to rest on his chest. His heart was racing, the beat pounding against my palm like a drum.

He nodded, his gaze never leaving mine. "More than anything."

With that, he claimed my mouth in a kiss that left me breathless. His tongue explored my mouth with a hunger that matched the ache in my core. As our bodies pressed closer together, the sounds of our passion grew louder - the wet smack of our lips, the harsh gasps for air, the rustle of clothing being pushed aside.

My fingers found their way to the button of his jeans, eager to free the cock that deep down I knew i'd want to explore one day. It sprang to life in my hand, hot and heavy, and I couldn't resist the urge to stroke it. Joey groaned into the kiss, his hips bucking against my touch.

We broke apart, both of us panting. Joey's eyes were dark with need, and the sight of his arousal made me even wetter. "you're so beautiful," he murmured, his voice thick with desire.

I felt a blush creep up my neck as I leaned in to kiss him again, feeling his cock pulse in my hand. The room was a cocoon of heat and want, the air thick with the scent of our need for each other.

Larissa

NINE

....

A few days passed. The old farmhouse loomed ahead, its dilapidated facade casting long shadows across the overgrown yard, a haunting silhouette against the twilight sky. The weight of what I was about to reveal pressed down on me like the oppressive air before a violent storm. But first, I had to lure Joey here without raising suspicion.

Earlier that day, I had texted him a deceptively casual message: "Hey Joey! I've got something huge to show you at the farmhouse. Consider it a live-action episode straight out of your favourite true crime podcast! Don't forget your detective cap!"

I knew that would reel him in. Joey always fancied himself an amateur sleuth, boasting he could outsmart even the sharpest tv detectives. Little did he realise, he was walking into a macabre mystery he could never solve.

When Joey arrived, morbid curiosity danced in his eyes. I could practically see the cogs turning as he surveyed the scene. "so, what's the big revelation? Are we investigating a murder?" he queried, his tone an unsettling blend of jest and gravity.

"Or committing one," I retorted, my feeble attempt to diffuse the suffocating tension.

He arched an eyebrow, a wry smirk playing at the corners of his mouth. "you're joking, right? Because premeditated murder seems a tad above my pay grade."

"Calm down, it's all under control," I countered, forcing a hollow laugh. "but we could use some excitement, don't you think?"

I crafted a text that dripped with false sincerity, luring Larissa to the farmhouse under the guise of reconciliation. "hey, Larissa! Can we talk? Joey really wants to clear the air and move past everything. He misses you, and I think it's time to put all this behind us. Meet us at the farmhouse? It'll be like old times. Just us three, hashing things out and maybe even sharing some laughs." I could almost hear the wheels turning in her head as she read my message, the flicker of hope igniting her curiosity. Little did she know, this was no heartfelt reunion; it was a carefully laid trap, where the stakes were higher than she could ever imagine.

Anticipation hung heavy in the air as we made our way to the farmhouse. The flickering fluorescent bulb inside cast shadows that danced along the walls, heightening the pervasive sense of dread. Steeling myself, I took a deep breath before confessing my darkest secret to Joey. "you remember Jessica and Leah, right? I told you about them before.well, I..." My voice faltered, the enormity of my admission hanging in the air like a noose. "I killed them. Slowly. While they begged for mercy."

Joey's eyes widened in horrified disbelief, the gruesome revelation sinking in. "What the fuck? Why would you do that?"

I stepped closer, my voice dropping to a menacing whisper. "they were a threat. To me."

His gaze fell, the sickening reality setting in. "So you just...snuffed them out? Like they were nothing?"

"There's more," I replied, sensing his rising panic as the storm swirled outside. "I need you to understand the necessity. This is bigger than anything"

Before he could respond, the door creaked open and Larissa stumbled inside, her face a ghastly shade of pale, rivulets of crimson dripping from the gash on her arm. "Joey!" She screamed, her voice shrill with terror as she collapsed onto the dirty floor

In a flash, Joey lunged for her assuming she was a stranger. Panicking, he grabbed a nearby set of shears, its razor-sharp blades glinting in the light. I must change that bulb. He swung wildly, the steel just grazing her flesh. She crumpled, eyes rolling back, a marionette with cut strings.

"Larissa!" I shouted, but Joey stood petrified, frozen by the horror of his actions.

"What have I done?" he stammered, his voice quavering with shock and disbelief. "I...I didn't mean to..."

"Calm the fuck down," I growled, stepping towards him, struggling to contain the maelstrom. "It's just a flesh wound. Christ, she'll survive."

Through gritted teeth, I laughed "I'll finish...what I started..." a grotesque smile twisted on my face face, my words dripping with venomous determination.

"Finish what, exactly?" Joey choked out, eyes darting frantically between us, caught in the crossfire of betrayal. "What the hell is happening?"

Urgency coursing through my veins, I pulled out my phone. "Look," I hissed, shoving the screen in his face. Scrolling through the damning instagram posts, Larissa's infidelity stared back at us— a lurid trail of incriminating evidence. "She fucked you over. You were right to fuck me and get your own back."

His face crumpled, anguish and heartbreak etched into every line. "I thought...I thought we were in love," he whispered hoarsely.

"Love doesn't fuck each other over," I spat, desperation seeping into my voice. "but i'll clean up this mess. You just need to trust me."

He was trembling now, confusion and fear clouding his vision. "what if she talks? What if..."

"She won't," I cut him off, my tone sharp as the shears Joey had dropped. "let me handle it, okay?"

In that moment, Joey snapped, his breathing ragged and shallow. "I can't do this! I can't be a part of this!" he stumbled back, knocking into the counter, sending a bottle of bleach crashing to the floor. The cap burst off, noxious fumes filling the room.

"No!" I yelled, grabbing for the bottle as it slipped through his shaking fingers. "don't!"

But it was too late. In a moment of sheer despair, Joey raised the bottle to his lips, the caustic liquid sloshing inside like a toxic tide. "I'm sorry..." he whispered, a tear rolling down his cheek before he chugged the bleach in one desperate gulp.

"Joey!" I screamed, my heart pounding against my ribcage, bile rising in my throat.

He collapsed, writhing on the ground, foam and blood dribbling from his mouth as he convulsed, the bleach eating away at his insides. I watched helplessly, hot tears scalding my face, as he choked and sputtered, the light in his eyes fading until he lay still.

I stared at Joey's lifeless body, the crushing weight of reality slamming into me like a tidal wave. This wasn't how it was meant to go. I had orchestrated every detail—my alibi, my airtight control over the situation—but now, I was left alone amidst the carnage, the bitter taste of failure rising in my throat.

Larissa's pained voice cut through the heavy silence, a weak mockery of triumph. "You really thought...you were in control?"

I turned to face her, a twisted revelation slithering into my mind. I had woefully underestimated the chaos I had unleashed, the darkness that had taken root and festered in the very marrow of my being.

"Maybe I should have finished you myself," I murmured, a cold resolve settling over me like a shroud. No more games, no more hesitation. The night had only just begun, and I would see it through to its bloody end.

With each beat of my heart, the suffocating weight of my choices pressed down on my chest, a grim reminder of the point of no return. The old farmhouse, once a refuge, had become the haunting stage for my most sadistic acts, each room bearing witness to my escalating brutality.

I knew this time I wanted to kill in a different way. That watching Joey falling to the ground had made me want to kill Larissa in a way I hadn't before.

The sound of the roosters crowing outside the farmhouse echoed. I had felt sorry for Larissa the other night, but now, she was nothing more than a symbol of my frustration, a blemish on the canvas of my life that needed to be eradicated as I look towards joey's lifeless body. I could see the ropes hanging from the ceiling beams, remnants of my father's hard work, and a tool that would soon serve a much darker purpose. I felt a twisted sense of excitement as I approached her, I had managed to knock her out with a swift whack to the head with the shears. She was bound with the same ropes we had used to secure the hay, her wrists and ankles tightly fastened, leaving her utterly helpless and exposed. Larissa was always the feisty one, so I knew she would put up more of a fight than Jessica and Leah had. I relished the challenge she would present.

As I began to strip her naked, her eyes fluttered open, and she immediately began to struggle, her body writhing against the unforgiving restraints. Her breasts heaved with each panicked breath she took, her eyes wild with fear. "You sick bastard," she spat, her voice thick with anger. But unlike the others, I had no desire to hear her pleas, no thrill in her fear. The only thing I wanted was for her to feel one last shred of pleasure before the end. I knew it was twisted, but I wanted her to remember this moment, to feel something other than pain before she left this world.

So, I started to kiss her neck, feeling her pulse quicken under my lips. She squirmed, trying to escape my touch, but I was insistent. I had never wanted to have sex with Larissa, not in the way I had with the others, but now, as I looked into her eyes filled with a mix of hatred and confusion, I found myself feeling something I hadn't expected—a strange, morbid affection. Ignoring the venom in her voice, I trailed my tongue down her body, my eyes never leaving hers.

When I reached her pussy, I took a moment to appreciate the sight—pink and swollen, a stark contrast to the cold, unforgiving ropes. I licked her, slow and deliberate, watching as her screams grew louder, her body bucking against the restraints. Her screams were not of arousal but of pure, unbridled fear. The taste of her filled my mouth, a bitter sweetness that only heightened the depravity of the situation. Her eyes searched mine for some shred of humanity, but all she found was the cold, unfeeling gaze of the monster I had become. Her legs tightened around my head, trying to push me away, but I was relentless, determined to give her what I thought she needed—what I thought she deserved. Her nails dug into the wooden beams above her, the sound of her desperate struggle echoing through the empty farmhouse.

With a sigh of resignation, I reached for the shears that I had left on the dusty wooden table nearby, their gleaming metal a stark contrast to the soft flesh of Larissa's bound form. Her eyes grew even wider, the realisation of her impending doom seeping in like the cold, early morning light that filtered through the cracks in the barn's wooden walls. She thrashed and screamed, her voice hoarse from the futile struggle against the ropes, the sound of her desperation a symphony to my ears. I approached her with the shears, the cold steel a comforting weight in my hand, a tool that would bring her the final release she so desperately craved. Her eyes never left mine, and I could see the understanding in them—she knew what was about to happen.

Her breaths grew ragged as I positioned the shears around her neck, the metal pressing into her soft, warm flesh. I could feel the rapid pulse of her carotid artery, a rhythm that seemed to match the beat of my own blackened heart. I whispered in her ear, "This will be quick, Larissa," as if the promise of swift death could ease the pain of what I was about to do. She spat at me, her saliva landing on my cheek, but I didn't flinch. Instead, I tightened my grip and, with one swift, brutal motion, I sliced through the rope that had held her ankles together. She kicked out, a last-ditch effort to escape her fate, but she was too late. I stepped back, admiring the fear and anger that danced in her eyes, a masquerade of emotions that only served to make her more beautiful in her final moments.

With a sadistic smile, I raised the shears once more, this time bringing them down to the base of her throat. The blade was sharp, slicing through her skin and the rope that held her wrists as if it were nothing more than a piece of thread. Her eyes widened in shock as the ropes fell away, and she felt the cold steel press against her. I watched as the last vestiges of her hope drained away, leaving only the stark reality of the situation. Her final words were a garbled scream as I tightened the shears, severing the rope that had held her arms apart. I stepped back, allowing her to drop to the floor, the ropes around her ankles still in place. She gasped for breath, her hands clutching at her throat, trying to hold back the inevitable.

But I wasn't done yet. With a final, cruel twist, I straddled her, one knee pressing into her chest as I took her face in my hands. "Look at me, Larissa," I demanded, and she did, her eyes filled with a mix of anger and despair. "look at the monster you've created," I whispered, and then, with a swift, savage motion, I brought the shears up to her throat. Her eyes never left mine as I slit her throat, the warm spray of blood painting my face as her lifeblood gushed out. Her body convulsed, a macabre dance of death beneath me, and I felt a strange sense of satisfaction as the light in her eyes began to fade.

The farmhouse was silent once more, the only sound the distant crowing of the roosters and the slow drip of Larissa's lifeblood onto the straw-covered floor. I stared down at her, feeling a strange mix of emotions—relief, anger, and a twisted form of affection that I couldn't quite name. But as her eyes glazed over, and her body grew still, I knew that I had done what needed to be done.

Echoes of Regret

TEN

As I stood in the dim light of the farmhouse, the silence was so heavy it felt like a thick blanket smothering me. Joey lay there, still and lifeless, and the weight of what had just happened pressed down on my chest like a stubborn raccoon refusing to leave my porch. I could hardly breathe, my mind racing with thoughts I never thought I'd have to confront.

I never imagined I would feel this way about Joey. He was supposed to be my partner in crime, not in the murderous way either, the one who took the dull away and turned it into an escapade. I had chased that high, convinced it made me feel alive. But now, staring at the empty shell that was once him, I realised how tragically wrong I had been. The adrenaline had numbed my feelings, made me reckless, and in my pursuit of excitement, I had lost something precious—someone precious.

Memories flooded my mind like a chaotic slideshow. The way he laughed, that goofy smile that could light up the darkest corners of my heart, and the spark in his eyes when he talked about his ridiculous dreams of becoming a professional pancake flipper. I had always brushed aside the idea of loving him, never thinking he could mean so much to me. But here I was, utterly shattered by the truth that I had let my obsession with danger take him away from me. I didn't want to imagine life without him, didn't want to think about how I had discarded the girls before him like yesterday's takeout. But Joey was different. He was real, he was mine, and I couldn't bear the thought of doing the same to him.

Panic surged through me like a quick shot of espresso. I had to call the police, had to do the right thing, but my hands trembled as I picked up my phone. What would I say? "Hey, uh, I just accidentally turned a girls boyfriend into an ex-boyfriend?" The idea felt absurd, and yet here I was, a living paradox. The adrenaline that usually fuelled my reckless decisions now left me paralysed, caught in a web of guilt and despair. I didn't want to be a killer. I didn't want to be the person who could just walk away, leaving him behind like I had done before.

But deep down lurked something darker than guilt: desperation. An idea sparked—a plan formed amidst thus tremendous carnage that would allow life to continue untouched by tragedy…at least for a little while longer. I glanced around at our makeshift sanctuary—the farmhouse reeked not only of hay but also regret—and quickly steeled myself for what needed doing next. Larissa's body lay cold beside Joey's. Grabbing some of the same old feed buckets typically reserved for slopping pigs—our muddy companions who eagerly awaited their delicious meals—I carefully manoeuvred her body into one without looking too closely at her face; focusing instead on maintaining composure while ignoring every ounce of humanity clawing at me from within. "Sorry girls," I muttered softly under breath before shuffling outside towards their pen—a whimsical thought crossed my mind: perhaps they'd appreciate an unexpected feast today? As grizzly as it sounded even to myself—my stomach churned—but practicality won out over sentimentality once more; no time for second-guessing or remorseful contemplation now. After disposing of Larissa's remains (with remarkable efficiency), cleaning up became paramount before anyone noticed anything amiss—the bleach bottle gleamed malevolently under fading sunlight as if beckoning disaster closer still—but careful steps ensured no trace remained behind apart from echoes lingering long after chaos subsided.

Overnight hours melted into days until routine returned somewhat unscathed—I planned to arrive back at our farm three days later as though nothing extraordinary transpired amongst us during those sleepless nights spent haunted by memories too vivid to forget entirely yet blurred enough not quite distinct anymore either… When daybreak arrived brightened by golden rays spilling across the sky, life was ripe with potential mischief again—I approached the days slowly, forging normalcy despite unease creeping beneath my skin until finally finding myself standing once more before Joey's motionless form sprawled awkwardly against the farmhouse floor.

The air was thick, a sickly-sweet perfume of decay wrapping around me like an unwelcome hug. My stomach twisted in protest, a rebellious beast ready to unleash its contents at any moment. I fought the urge to hurl, forcing my face into a mask of composure. This was my masterpiece, a careful symphony of deception, and I couldn't let it unravel now.

With a deep, shuddering breath that felt more like a gasp for life, I steeled myself for my performance. My heart thudded like a drummer with a caffeine addiction, beating out a frantic rhythm against my ribs, drowning out the silent horror that unfolded before me. I had to sell this. I had to convince them I was a victim, not the twisted architect of this grim scenario.

I approached Joey's body with all the grace of a newborn giraffe, each step echoing unnervingly in the farmhouse's stillness. I paused, feigning a moment of horrified discovery that would make even the greatest actors proud. My eyes widened, shock and terror flawlessly etched onto my face in a masterpiece of overacting. Then, with all the flair of a Broadway star, I let out a scream—a high-pitched wail that sliced through the morning like a knife through butter, raw and animalistic, part of me genuinely terrified by what I had done. I crumpled to my knees, clutching my chest as if I had just survived a surprise kidney punch.

But that scream? Not entirely false. A sliver of real fear, a sharp jab of guilt, pricked at my conscience, reminding me that the smell of decay was more than just a bad aftershave. Yet I pressed on, my performance fuelled by a primal need for survival—or perhaps just an overwhelming desire to not wind up in a cell next to someone named "Big Bertha."

With trembling hands, I fumbled for my phone, its cold metal contrasting sharply with the clammy sweat pooling in my palms. My fingers, clumsy and shaking like a leaf in a windstorm, struggled to dial the emergency number. As I spoke to the dispatcher, my voice was a quivering whisper barely drowning out the furious pounding of my heart, which seemed to be auditioning for a horror film soundtrack. I painted a vivid picture of a peaceful morning shattered by a gruesome discovery, a scene of unimaginable suicide that had left me traumatised and, dare I say, a little bit dramatic.

"He's... he's dead," I stammered, my voice catching in my throat, a convincing imitation of shock. "I found him like this... on the floor... There's... there's bleach....there is....please help" I paused, letting silence amplify the horror, before adding, with a theatrical sob worthy of an Oscar, "It smells... terrible. He's... he's been dead for a while, I think."

The dispatcher, calm and professional, offered soothing words like a warm cup of hot chocolate on a winter's day, her voice a calming balm against the truth swirling within me. But beneath my façade, a cold dread gnawed at my insides, like a rat with a vendetta. The charade was working, sure, but the weight of my secret clung to me like a persistent oil stain on my favourite shirt. The golden sunlight, once a beacon of hope, now felt like a cruel spotlight illuminating my carefully constructed lie. The game was afoot, and I was playing it perfectly—or at least that's what I kept telling myself as I knelt next to Joey, the unfortunate star of my story.

The sunlight streamed through the dusty windows of the farmhouse, casting a warm glow that felt almost ironic given the chill creeping up my spine."My friend… he had gone missing for a few days, and I just found him in my farmhouse. It smells… really bad. I think he might have had a mishap while cleaning. I don't know how long he's been like this."

The dispatcher's voice was calm and professional, but I could hear the underlying urgency. "Can you tell me exactly what you see? Is he conscious?"

"Uh, well, he's definitely not conscious," I replied, trying to keep my voice steady, though panic clawed at my throat. "I think he might be… deceased. He always joked about cleaning being the death of him, but I didn't think he meant it literally!" I laughed weakly, the absurdity of the situation crashing over me like a cold wave. "I mean, who knew bleach could be so deadly? It's like he took 'spring cleaning' to a whole new level!"

The dispatcher paused briefly, probably trying to process the bizarre mix of humour and horror in my words. "Stay where you are. Help is on the way."

"Great," I replied, my voice faltering as I leaned against the wall, trying to steady myself. "I guess it's just me and the ghost of Joey now. It's going to be an interesting few days."

As I waited, I couldn't shake the feeling that somewhere, somehow, Joey would have found a way to make this whole mess into a darkly comedic story. "You always said life was a comedy," I whispered to the empty room, hoping he was listening. "Guess you really meant it."

The wait felt intense, each tick of the clock amplifying the stillness in the farmhouse. I paced back and forth, my mind swirling with a chaotic mix of thoughts. "What would the police think when they arrived?" I wondered. Would they see me as the concerned friend or the potential suspect in a bizarre and tragic narrative? I could almost hear the ominous notes of a true crime documentary playing in the background, complete with dramatic music. I must write about this when I get back home, it's superb.

Finally, the sound of sirens broke the heavy silence, their wails growing louder as they approached. Relief washed over me, but it was quickly followed by a fresh wave of anxiety. I took a deep breath, trying to compose myself. I still felt like I was caught in some twisted soap mother used to watch, but this was far from a laughing matter.

The door burst open, and two officers stepped in, their demeanour serious but not unkind. "Miss, we received a call about a possible emergency," one of them said, scanning the room with a practiced eye. His partner, a woman with a steely gaze, followed suit, her expression revealing nothing.

"Uh, yes, that's me," I stammered, pointing vaguely toward the living room. "It's my friend, Joey. He's… well, he's not really… alive anymore." I gestured awkwardly, feeling like I was directing traffic.

The officers exchanged a glance before moving with purpose into the farmhouse. I trailed behind, my heart pounding in my chest. As they stepped into the room, I watched their faces shift from concern to disbelief. The male officer knelt down next to Joey, while the female one began assessing the surroundings.

"Is he…?" I started, but the words caught in my throat. I didn't want to say it. The reality was too harsh, and saying it out loud felt like I was sealing my own fate.

"Stay back, please," the female officer instructed gently but firmly, her attention focused on Joey's still form. "We need to check for signs of life first."

The male officer reached for his radio, speaking into it with calm authority. "Dispatch, we have an unresponsive male in the farmhouse. Requesting medics on the scene." He looked over at me, his expression softening slightly. "Can you tell us what happened?"

I took a deep breath, trying to find the words. "I hadn't heard from him in days, and I just figured he was busy with chores or something," I explained, my voice trembling. "When I got here, it smelled awful, and then I saw him—next to a bottle of bleach, like he was trying to clean up before the apocalypse or something."

The officers exchanged another look, and I felt a pang of embarrassment. "I didn't think he would actually… you know, go that far. He always joked about cleaning being the death of him, but I thought it was just a joke. I didn't think he'd take it literally!"

The female officer nodded, her expression softening further. "It's okay. It sounds like you were worried about him and came to check in. That's what friends do."

Just then, the medics arrived, rushing into the room with their equipment. I stepped back, feeling like a spectator in my own life as they began assessing the situation with practiced efficiency. The reality of what was happening settled heavily on my shoulders. "This is really happening," I thought, a mix of disbelief and sorrow swirling inside me.

As the medics worked, I caught snippets of their conversation, the technical jargon swirling around me. "Decomposition… possible poisoning… need to alert the coroner…" Each phrase felt like a punch to the gut, a grim reminder of the finality of it all.

After what felt like a lifetime, the female officer turned to me, her expression serious. "We're going to need you to come with us to the station to give a formal statement. It's just a standard procedure, okay?"

I nodded, feeling numb. "Sure, I'll do whatever you need." I glanced back at Joey one last time, the laughter and camaraderie we had shared flooding my mind. "I'm so sorry, buddy," I whispered under my breath, wishing I could turn back time and save him from this fate.

As I stepped out into the sunlight, the weight of the day pressed down on me like a heavy fog. I could only hope that somewhere, Joey was shaking his head, laughing at the sheer absurdity of it all, maybe even rolling his eyes at my dramatics. "Life really is a comedy," I thought, choking back tears. "And I'm left to navigate the punchlines."

The drive to the police station felt like a montage from a low-budget thriller—my mind raced with a thousand chaotic thoughts, each more frantic than the last. It was the kind of surreal nightmare where you're being chased but can't seem to run, your legs feeling like they're stuck in molasses. "What if they start digging too deep?" I thought, gnawing on my lip. "What if they find out about… the other incidents?" The word "incidents" hung over me like a dark cloud, each syllable dripping with unwelcome memories.

As we pulled into the station, the building loomed ahead, stark and imposing, like a judge ready to deliver a life sentence. "Thanks for the ride, guys," I thought sarcastically, stepping out of the car. A knot of dread twisted tighter in my stomach, making me feel like I'd just swallowed a live frog. The officers led me inside, their expressions serious yet not unkind. I knew they were just doing their jobs, but the weight of their authority felt stifling—like being trapped under a giant, judgmental thumb.

Once inside, I was escorted to a small, dimly lit interrogation room that looked like it had been designed for maximum discomfort. A table sat in the centre, flanked by two metal chairs that had clearly seen better days—probably during the last decade's budget cuts. I hesitated before sitting down, suddenly acutely aware of how exposed I felt. The walls felt like they were closing in, and the shadows cast by the harsh overhead light seemed to creep closer, ready to ensnare me in their grasp like a bad horror movie.

"Just a few questions, and then you'll be free to go," the female officer said, her tone steady but lacking the warmth of a cosy blanket, its no wonder she got this job! She took a seat across from me, her partner leaning against the wall with his arms crossed, watching me with an intensity that made my skin crawl, as if I were a particularly fascinating fossil in a museum.

"Let's start from the beginning," she said, pulling out a notepad that looked like it had survived a few too many coffee spills. "How did you find Joey?"

I opened my mouth to respond, but my brain was still in a state of panic, as if it had taken a wrong turn somewhere down the rabbit hole of anxiety. "Uh, well, you see..." I stammered, trying to recall the details without sounding like a complete lunatic. "I hadn't heard from him in days, and I figured he was just busy with his... uh, chores."

"Chores," she repeated, jotting down my words with a seriousness that made me feel like I was confessing to a crime. "What kind of chores?"

"Y'know, the usual—mucking out stalls, counting sheep, probably plotting a sheep rebellion," I responded, trying to inject a bit of humour into the situation. "He always joked about how he was the 'shepherd of the sheep'—but honestly, I think they were the ones shepherding him with all the trouble they caused he loved helping me at the farm."

The officer stared at me with the kind of expression that suggested my sheep-related quips were not going to earn me any points. "And when you went to check on him, what did you find?" she asked, her pen poised for a dramatic reveal.

I took a deep breath, my stomach churning at the memory. "Well, when I got there, I thought he might be cleaning up or something, but instead, it smelled like a chemistry lab explosion mixed with, I don't know, regret? I opened the door, and there he was, just... not moving.

Next to a bottle of bleach, of all things. I mean, who knew cleaning could be so deadly?"

The female officer nodded, her expression inscrutable. "And you didn't think to call anyone sooner?"

"Honestly, I thought he was just deep-cleaning the barn or binge-watching something ridiculous," I admitted, feeling a mix of shame and frustration. "I never imagined I'd find him like that. I mean, he always joked about cleaning being the death of him, I told the dispatcher on the phone , but I didn't think he'd take it literally!"

Her eyes narrowed slightly, and I felt the weight of her scrutiny. "You seem awfully familiar with his habits," she noted, her pen scratching across the paper. "Are you sure there's nothing else you want to tell us?"

My heart raced. "Nothing else! Just a friend checking on another friend!" I blurted, the words tumbling out awkwardly. "I swear, if I had known he was on a cleaning spree that could rival an episode of 'Hoarders,' I would have intervened sooner!"

The tension in the room was palpable, and I could feel the shadows closing in tighter around me. What if they started asking questions that hit too close to home? What if they unearthed secrets I had buried deep beneath layers of guilt and denial? My mind raced, and I silently pleaded with the universe for a distraction—any distraction—to steer this conversation away from the dark corners of my past.

The male officer shifted, his gaze piercing. "You seem awfully calm for someone who just found their friend like that."

I swallowed hard, my heart pounding in my chest. "I didn't know what else to do. I panicked!" Panic wasn't the only thing I felt. The thought of them unearthing my past, the dark secrets that lay like hidden landmines, sent shivers down my spine. I could almost hear the whispers of suspicion creeping into the room, like an unwelcome guest who overstayed their welcome.

"What do you mean by 'accident'?" the female officer pressed, her pen poised over her notepad. "Are you suggesting he might have…"

"No! I mean, yes, but not like that!" I stammered, feeling the walls close in even further. "I just think he might have been cleaning and… things got out of hand."

The officers exchanged a glance, and my stomach twisted in knots. What if they started piecing together the truth? What if they began to connect the dots between Joey's unfortunate demise and the other two incidents that had haunted my past? The thought made me feel sick. I had been so careful, but now everything felt precarious, like a house of cards ready to tumble down.

"Let's talk about your relationship with Joey," the female officer continued, her tone shifting slightly. "How would you describe it?"

"We were friends," I said, trying to keep my voice steady. "He helped me out on the farm. We had some good times—joked around a lot. Nothing out of the ordinary." I felt the tension in the room grow thicker, like a noose tightening around my neck.

"Did you ever have any disagreements? Any reasons for conflict?" she asked, her gaze unwavering.

I shook my head vigorously, my mind racing. "No, absolutely not! We got along well. He was like family to me." Family. The word felt heavy on my tongue, a reminder of the bonds I had shattered before.

"Do you know if he had any problems? Financial issues? Relationships gone wrong?" the male officer interjected, his voice steady but probing.

"No! Nothing like that!" I blurted out, my heart racing. "He was just a good guy!"

I had thoughts of mentioning Larissa but I didn't want her name in the picture, this was terrifying enough and I rarely feel terror.

The questions continued, each one prying deeper into my thoughts, and I felt the weight of my secrets pressing down on me. The fear of getting caught for the other two murders loomed like a dark cloud overhead, threatening to burst and drown me in its storm. I could feel the officers' scrutiny like a spotlight, illuminating the shadows of my past that I desperately wanted to keep buried.

As the questions wore on, I realised that I was in a precarious position. The officers had control over the farmhouse now, and with it, they held the power to uncover everything I had tried so hard to forget. I just needed to keep my story straight, to maintain the façade of being the worried friend caught in a tragic circumstance. But the fear that they would see through my carefully constructed lie lingered in the air like a heavy fog, and I could only hope that the truth would remain hidden long enough for me to slip away from this nightmare.

    Finally, after what felt like an eternity, they let me go. I walked out of the station into the crisp night air, feeling the cool breeze on my face like a slap of reality. I needed to get out of here, to put some distance between myself and the prying eyes of the law. Without wasting a second, I headed home to pack.

Blackpool

ELEVEN

The chilly sea breeze of Blackpool slapped my cheeks as I stepped out of the taxi, my luggage rolling behind me like a reluctant pet. The neon lights of the amusement park twinkled in the distance, winking at me as if to say, "Welcome to pandemonium; we have cotton candy and questionable decisions!" I had never been here before, but the town's reputation as a chaotic kaleidoscope of joy was exactly what I needed to shake off the dust of my past. Plus, where else could I potentially win a giant stuffed dinosaur?

My heart raced as I fished my phone out of my pocket and with a trembling thumb, I powered it down. It felt like the declaration of independence, a silent scream into the void of my existence. No more calls from Bridgefield, no more texts that chilled my blood, no more emojis that made me want to throw my phone out the window. The world outside my little bubble was a minefield of pain and danger, but here, in this tacky wonderland, I could finally breathe. And eat fish and chips without judgment!

The Travelodge stood before me, a beacon of budget charm nestled between a kebab shop and a convenience store that boasted of being open 24/7. I checked in with a smile that felt more like a grimace, the clerk's polite demeanour doing its best to hide the fact that she was probably wondering how someone could look so disheveled yet determined. My room, when I finally entered, was a mix of old and new, with the faint scent of disinfectant mingling with the stale remnants of cigarettes—just the right ambiance for existential musings! It wasn't much, but it felt like a sanctuary—a place where I could lay my head and not fear the whispers of the shadows... or the sound of my own snoring.

The TV in the corner was a relic from another era, its screen flickering to life as I flipped through the channels. I found solace in the mind-numbing banality of daytime talk shows and adverts for kitchen gadgets that I would never use but still felt the urge to buy. The laugh track of a sitcom filled the small space, a stark contrast to the symphony of screams and sirens that typically serenaded me back home. For the first time in what felt like forever, I felt a strange sensation bubble up from my chest—a laugh, awkward and rusty, but genuine. It escaped my lips like a forgotten melody, surprising me with its warmth. I even caught myself chuckling at a cat video—my new favourite form of therapy.

But as the days stretched on, the shadows grew restless. My mind began to play tricks on me, whispering the names of those I had left behind. The fear that had been my constant companion for so long became a muted scream in the back of my thoughts, growing louder with each passing minute, threatening to shatter the fragile peace I had constructed. It was like my brain had turned into a karaoke machine, and the only songs it knew were the sad ones.

The phone in my bag called to me like a seductive siren, promising connection to the real world, promising relief from the isolation. But I knew the price of that relief was steep. With trembling hands, I wrapped the phone in a towel—because nothing says "I'm serious about my escape" like a mini spa treatment for my electronics—and placed it at the bottom of the mini fridge. The cold steel door became a fortress, keeping my tether to the outside world at bay, along with the leftover takeout I probably wouldn't eat.

The silence was deafening. The humorous banter of the TV hosts morphed into a cacophony of accusations, and my thoughts spiralled into the unspeakable things I had done, the lives I had left in my wake. The laughter from the screen felt like a taunt, a cruel jest at my attempt to find refuge in this garish seaside town. I missed the cobblestone streets of Bridgefield, the comfort of the known, even the shadows that were familiar. At least I knew where the potholes were back home.

The tension grew, a palpable force that wrapped around me, suffocating in its grip. I hadn't realised how much I relied on the constant background noise of my old life to drown out the voices that haunted me. But here, in the quiet of my Travelodge room, they were all I could hear, and let me tell you, they were terrible at karaoke.

My eyes darted to the clock on the wall, ticking away the seconds with a metronome's cruel precision. Each tick was a reminder of the time I had wasted trying to escape, of the moments I had lost in my futile pursuit of peace. The room felt smaller, the air thicker with each inhale, my chest tightening like a vice. I could almost hear the waves crashing against the shore outside, a rhythmic reminder of the world that continued to spin, indifferent to my struggles. As the clock continued its relentless ticking, I found myself staring at the ceiling, contemplating the patterns in the faded wallpaper. Were those flowers or just a sad attempt at modern art? I couldn't tell. My thoughts wandered to the amusement park outside, where laughter mingled with the sounds of the rides. I could almost hear the shrieks of delight from the roller coasters, the screams of joy that felt so foreign to me now.

With a sudden burst of spontaneity, I swung my legs over the side of the bed and stood up. "Why not?" I muttered to myself. If I was going to spend the weekend in this carnival of chaos, I might as well join the circus. I didn't exactly have a clown costume, but I figured my current state of dishevelment would fit right in.

I stepped out of my Travelodge sanctuary, the fresh sea air filling my lungs and giving me a rush of courage. The neon lights beckoned me closer, and I felt like a moth drawn to the flame. I walked past the kebab shop, its enticing aroma wafting through the air, and made a mental note to return. After all, a proper adventure requires sustenance, right?

As I entered the amusement park, the atmosphere hit me like a wave of nostalgia. Children screamed in delight, couples wandered hand in hand, and groups of friends laughed over their cotton candy. I could feel the weight of my worries lifting, replaced by the intoxicating buzz of excitement. I ambled past games of chance, each one shouting for attention with promises of oversized plush toys.

I caught sight of a booth offering a shooting game with a giant stuffed dinosaur as the grand prize. A surge of determination washed over me. "I'm getting that dinosaur," I declared, marching up to the booth like I was about to face a dragon. The attendant raised an eyebrow, clearly skeptical of my chances, but I was undeterred.

With the first shot, I missed. The second shot hit the edge of the target. But then—boom!—the third shot hit dead centre, followed by a second and a third. I could hardly believe my luck! I threw my arms up in triumph, feeling like a warrior who had just slayed a beast. With each shot, I could feel the laughter bubbling up inside me, almost drowning out the whispers of doubt.

"Congratulations!" the attendant said, reluctantly handing me the enormous plush dinosaur. It was far too big for me to carry comfortably, but I didn't care. I hugged it close, revealing in the ridiculousness of the situation. I felt lighter, freer—like I could float right out of the park.

I wandered through the attractions, the dinosaur swinging from side to side in my arms, and I couldn't help but smile at the absurdity of it all. I stopped at a food stall and ordered the most cliché meal I could think of: fish and chips drenched in vinegar. As I sat down, I took a moment to appreciate the scene before me—a kaleidoscope of joy, chaos, and delicious grease.

The taste was heavenly, a burst of flavour and warmth that made my heart swell. I even offered a few fries to a seagull that landed nearby, which promptly snatched them and squawked indignantly at me as if I had insulted its dignity. "Hey, no need to be rude!" I laughed, feeling a strange kinship with the bird.

As the sun began to set, casting a golden hue over the park, I found myself perched on a bench, my dinosaur by my side, soaking in the atmosphere. Laughter echoed around me, and I realised I hadn't felt this lighthearted in years. The shadows that had loomed so heavily in my mind were now just distant whispers, overshadowed by the joy of spontaneity.

But then, as if on cue, my thoughts turned back to my phone, buried at the bottom of the mini fridge. I felt a pang of guilt for leaving that part of my life behind, as if I was betraying the people who cared about me. But in this moment, I also understood that sometimes you need to step away from reality to reclaim a piece of yourself.

With the dinosaur nestled in my lap, I made a silent promise to myself. I would find a way to balance my past with this newfound sense of freedom. Maybe I didn't need to answer every call or respond to every message. Maybe I could just be—here, in this moment, enjoying the chaos of life without the weight of expectation.

As I watched the sunset paint the sky in vibrant colours, I knew this weekend in Blackpool was just the beginning. I hadn't solved all my problems, but I had taken the first step toward reclaiming my joy. And who knew? Maybe next, I'd try my hand at the roller coaster. After all, life was about embracing the ups and downs, and I was more than ready for the ride. As the vibrant colours of the sunset faded into the encroaching darkness, I felt a pull in my chest, an unwelcome reminder that my little escape in Blackpool had a ticking clock. I looked at my giant stuffed dinosaur, a ridiculous yet comforting companion, and knew that my time here was coming to an end. The laughter around me, the joy I had momentarily captured, felt fragile, like sand slipping through my fingers. It was time to face the real world again, for better or worse.

But honestly, who would've thought a giant plush T-Rex would become my emotional support dinosaur? I could almost hear it whispering, "Don't worry, I've got your back—unless we run into any actual dinosaurs."

I reluctantly made my way back to the Travelodge, dragging my plush dinosaur behind me like it was a shield against whatever awaited me back home. The moment I stepped into my room, the familiar silence enveloped me, a stark contrast to the joyous chaos I had just left. I approached the mini fridge, my heart racing as I contemplated switching on my phone. It felt like a lifeline, yet also a noose, and I wasn't entirely sure which one would be tighter.

With a deep breath, I powered it on. The screen lit up, and my stomach twisted into a pretzel as I saw the notification: 16 missed calls from a private number. My insides flipped like a carnival ride, and I felt a wave of nausea wash over me. I clicked through to my voicemail, my pulse quickening with each beep. The first voicemail played, and my breath caught in my throat as I heard the voice of PC Harrison, the officer who had been on Joey's case.

"Uh, hello, this is PC Harrison," he said, his voice steady but laced with an urgency that sent chills down my spine. "I need you to come to the station as soon as possible. There's been an update regarding Joey's death. I can't discuss it over the phone. Please, it's important."

An update? My mind spiralled into a frenzy. What did that mean? Was it an update on the case or an update on my life choices? I felt like a character in a bad horror movie, waiting for the twist that would send me into a panic. My fingers trembled as I replayed the message, trying to extract some hidden meaning from his words. I felt as if I were teetering on the edge of a cliff, with nothing but darkness below. And let's be real, I wasn't wearing my best shoes for cliff diving.

Suddenly, flashbacks assaulted me, each one more vivid than the last. The image of Joey, lying lifeless, flashed before my eyes, a haunting reminder of the night that had changed everything. The blood, the chaos, the frantic decision-making that had led me to this moment. My heart raced faster, and I could feel the weight of those memories pressing down on me like a particularly heavy sack of potatoes.

Then came the darker memories—faces of the dead bodies I had encountered, the lifeless forms that lingered in my mind like ghosts, taunting me. The pigs—oh God, the pigs—always lurking in the background, a reminder of sins I thought I had buried. And my family, their disappointed faces flashing in my mind's eye, a constant reminder of the trust I had shattered. I could practically hear them asking, "What's next? A reality show?"

My breath quickened, and a tightness gripped my chest. I staggered back, the room spinning around me as the panic took hold. What if they had found out? What if PC Harrison was calling to tell me I had been caught? My knees buckled, and I crumpled to the floor, the stuffed dinosaur rolling away like a casualty of war.

The walls felt like they were closing in, the shadows deepening around me. I was drowning in a sea of my own making, the reality closing in like a vise. I pressed my hands against my chest, willing my heart to slow down, to stop racing like a wild stallion. But the panic only intensified, each breath a struggle, each heartbeat a reminder of my impending doom.

"Get it together!" I whispered to myself, but the words felt hollow. The weight of my past loomed like a dark cloud, and nothing I did could shake it off. I could hear the echoes of police sirens in my mind, the clattering of handcuffs, the cold steel of reality pressing against my skin.

I fought to regain control, focusing on the giant dinosaur still in my peripheral vision, a silly reminder of the joy I had felt just hours ago. "This is not how it ends," I told myself. "You need to get out of here. You need to go home."

With trembling hands, I grabbed my phone again, staring at the missed calls. I had to go to the station, but I needed to prepare. I took a few deep breaths, forcing myself to ground in the present, reminding myself that I wasn't just a ghost from my past—I was still here, still standing, still capable of making choices.

As I rose to my feet, the panic began to ebb, replaced with a steely resolve. I would face whatever awaited me at the station. I would confront the truth, no matter how terrifying it was. I owed it to Joey, to the memories that haunted me, and to myself. With one last glance at the dinosaur, I grabbed my jacket, steeling myself for the confrontation that lay ahead.

"Okay, T-Rex," I said, giving my plush companion a determined nod, "let's go face my impending doom. And if I'm going down, I'm dragging you with me."

With that, I opened the door, ready to step back into the whirlwind of life outside, praying that I wouldn't end up as the star of my own tragic crime documentary. The world might be a chaotic mess, but I was about to find out just how deep the rabbit hole went.

As I stood there, heart pounding and the plush dinosaur clutched tightly in my arms, a thought flickered through my mind like a faulty light bulb: I wanted to get caught. Not today, not tomorrow, but someday. The adrenaline rush that had fuelled me through this chaotic existence couldn't last forever. I was beginning to realise that living life like a high-stakes game of hide-and-seek was exhausting.

Every time I slipped through the cracks, every time I evaded the gaze of the world outside, I felt that intoxicating thrill that came with it. It was a drug, pure and powerful—the kind that made your heart race and your senses heighten. But as I stood there, staring at the wall adorned with hastily scribbled notes and reminders of my past, I felt that familiar sense of dread creeping in. The high was starting to wear off.

I had tried to convince myself that writing those notes and sticking them around my room like some twisted prize would keep me grounded. Each reminder was a trophy, a testament to my survival, my cunning. But deep down, I knew that this facade couldn't hold up forever. The thrill of the chase, the game I was playing, was morphing into a cage, and I was the one who had locked myself inside.

There was a part of me that yearned for the release of being caught, the weight of the secrets I carried lifting off my shoulders. I imagined the moment when someone would finally see through the façade, when the carefully crafted illusion would shatter, and I'd be forced to confront the truth of who I was. There was a sick sense of relief in that thought, a longing for the chaos of being found out to replace the chaos of living in constant fear.

But not yet. I wasn't ready for that. I didn't want to be a headline or a cautionary tale. I wasn't ready to face the consequences of the choices I had made. The thought of being locked away, of losing my freedom, terrified me more than the idea of continuing this charade. I needed time to breathe, to figure out who I truly was beneath the weight of it all.

The adrenaline had become my lifeline, but I knew it was a double-edged sword. With every thrill, there was a cost, and eventually, I would have to settle the bill. I realised that being a serial killer wasn't a sustainable lifestyle; it was a ticking time bomb, and I was just waiting for it to go off. The fear of being caught loomed over me like a dark cloud, but part of me craved the clarity of confession, the catharsis of being seen.

As I looked down at my dinosaur, a ridiculous reminder of the joy I had felt just hours ago, I felt a flicker of hope. Maybe there was a way to find redemption without the need for punishment. Maybe I could confront my demons without the world needing to know every sordid detail.

"Not yet, T-Rex," I whispered, squeezing the plush toy tightly. "We're not ready to go down that road. I need to figure this out first."

With that thought lingering in my mind, I steeled myself for the confrontation awaiting me at the station. I had to face the music, but I also had to find a way to reclaim my life—before the game turned into a nightmare I couldn't escape. With a deep breath and my plush dinosaur clutched like a lifeline, I stepped out of my Travelodge room and into the cool night air. The streets of Blackpool buzzed with life, the sounds of laughter and chatter spilling from nearby pubs and amusement arcades. I felt like a ghost drifting through a world filled with joy, painfully aware of my own isolation.

I needed to get to the police station, and a taxi would do the trick. I flagged one down, its yellow glow illuminating my anxious face as I climbed in, the dinosaur awkwardly squeezed beside me. "To the police station, please," I said, trying to sound casual, but my voice trembled slightly. The driver nodded, and we pulled away, the familiar rhythm of the city fading into the background.

As we drove, the adrenaline surged within me—not from the thrill of evasion this time, but from the anticipation of what lay ahead. The police station loomed in my mind like a dark spectre. Each streetlight flickered by, and I could feel my heartbeat quicken, the weight of my secrets pressing down on me like an anchor. Was I ready for whatever awaited me there?

The taxi weaved through the bustling streets, and I caught glimpses of people enjoying the nightlife—couples laughing, families sharing moments of joy. I felt like an outsider looking in, my heart pounding in sync with the city's pulse. The driver occasionally glanced in the rear-view mirror, and I wondered if he could sense the turmoil churning within me. Did he know the weight of my past, the chaos I had tried so hard to escape?

As we approached the police station, a sense of dread settled in my stomach. The sterile smell of the air, the fluorescent lights buzzing overhead, and the weight of the truth that had nearly crushed me last time flooded back. I could practically hear PC Harrison's voice echoing in my mind, urging me to come in—his tone a mix of concern and urgency that sent chills down my spine.

The taxi came to a stop, and I took a moment to gather myself. I paid the driver, my hands shaking as I fumbled with the cash. "Keep the change," I muttered, eager to escape the confines of the cab. The plush dinosaur sat in my lap, a ridiculous yet oddly comforting reminder that I wasn't completely alone.

Stepping out into the cool night air, I glanced up at the imposing police station, its façade standing like a sentinel guarding my fate. This was it. I had to confront whatever awaited me inside.

With shaky hands, I approached the entrance, my heart pounding louder with each step. The door swung open with a creak, and I stepped into the stark, fluorescent-lit foyer. The atmosphere was thick with tension, and I could feel the weight of countless secrets hanging in the air.

"Can I help you?" a uniformed officer asked, his tone neutral but his gaze scrutinising.

"I'm here to see PC Harrison," I stammered, swallowing hard. "It's urgent."

"Right. Take a seat; I'll let him know you're here," the officer replied, nodding toward a row of uncomfortable plastic chairs. I took a seat, the plush dinosaur resting awkwardly in my lap.

As I waited, I couldn't shake the feeling of being watched—like I was a fly caught in a web, waiting for the spider to make its move. I glanced around the room, noting the flickering lights, the muted conversations of officers in the background, and the presence of a large poster warning about the dangers of drug abuse. It all felt surreal, like I had stumbled into a scene from a gritty drama.

Minutes felt like hours as I sat there, my mind racing with possibilities. Would they know? Would PC Harrison confront me about my past? My pulse quickened at the thought, and I squeezed the dinosaur tightly. Just as I was about to second-guess my decision, the door opened, and PC Harrison stepped through, his expression serious.

"Ms Thorne, are you ready to come through now?" he said, his tone brokering no argument. I nodded, my heart hammering in my chest as I followed him down a dimly lit corridor. Each step felt heavier, like I was walking toward my own execution.

As we reached his office, he motioned for me to sit. "We need to talk," he said, closing the door behind us. The air felt thick with tension, and I could sense that whatever he had to say would change everything.

But before he could begin, the phone on his desk rang, cutting through the charged silence. He glanced at the screen, his expression shifting to one of alarm. "I need to take this," he said, his voice tense as he picked up the receiver.

"Stay here," he added, his eyes locking onto mine. "We'll talk in a moment."

I nodded, but inside I felt a growing sense of unease. What was happening? Why did he look so worried? As he turned away to answer the call, my mind raced with possibilities, and the world outside the office faded into a blur.

PC Harrison stepped out of the room, the heavy door swinging shut with a finality that echoed in the silence, leaving me alone to grapple with the shit storm of my thoughts. Panic surged through me like a tidal wave, each wave crashing against the fragile structure of my mind, urging me to contemplate my life and the choices that had led me here. I could feel the walls closing in, the air thick with tension as I imagined a quick escape, a reckless sprint out of the building and into the night, where I could leave everything behind and never look back. What would it be like to run away from this suffocating reality, to vanish into a world untainted by the shadows of my past?

My thoughts spiralled toward the dark possibility that they might have found Larissa's blood, a gruesome reminder of the life that had unraveled before me. Just as I was spiralling deeper into despair, the door creaked open again, and there stood PC Harrison, a strange mix of amusement and incredulity on his face. He sniffled a laugh, shaking his head, and said it was just his missus asking him to pick up aubergine of all things on the way home, a trivial detail that felt utterly absurd in the gravity of the moment. But before I could process the absurdity of his return, the door burst open again, this time with a flurry as another police officer stormed in, disrupting the fragile calm and thrusting me back into the reality I so desperately wanted to escape.

"PC Harrison, we've got a situation," he said urgently. "It's about Joey."

My heart dropped, and the room spun around me. What did they know? What had happened? I felt a cold sweat break out on my brow as the implications of those words sank in.

And in that moment, with my heart racing and the weight of my past crashing down upon me, I realised that I was standing on the precipice of everything I had tried to escape. The truth was about to be revealed, and I was caught in the eye of the storm, unsure of what was about to unfold.

The officer's urgent voice faded into the background as I waited for the bombshell to drop, my stomach twisting in knots. The lines between past and present blurred, and I braced myself for the fallout that was about to come. Would I finally have to face the consequences of my actions? Would the truth set me free, or would it shatter everything I had built?

As the tension in the room mounted, I knew one thing for certain: whatever happened next would change everything. And I was right at the heart of it, teetering on the edge of my fate.

TWELVE

As PC Harrison and the other police officer stepped into the cramped room, sweat poured from every crevice of their uniforms, making it look like they had just come from an intense game of dodgeball in a sauna. The oppressive heat clung to the air, and I couldn't help but feel like I was wading through a thick fog of humidity. They wiped their brows dramatically, trying to regain their composure while Joey's phone buzzed ominously on the table, adding to the tension.

"Right, let's see what this phone has to say for itself," one of the officers said, squinting at the screen as if it held the secrets of the universe. They began scrolling through Joey's messages with the intense focus usually reserved for a detective uncovering a major plot twist.

As they sifted through the messages, they paused at a series of texts to a woman named Larissa. "Do you know her, Ms. Thorne?" one officer asked, glancing up at me with an expression that suggested they were on the brink of a breakthrough.

I shook my head, trying to sound casual, though my heart was racing. "No, I don't, but my name is mentioned a few times," I replied, attempting to shrug it off. Honestly, the way they kept calling me "Ms. Thorne" was starting to grate on my nerves. Did they not realise how annoying it was?

The officers exchanged a glance, a mix of concern and determination flashing across their faces. "We'll need to take your phone in as evidence, Ms. Thorne," PC Harrison said, his voice serious. "We're trying to piece together the circumstances of Joey's alleged suicide. We want to help his family through this difficult time."

At the mention of Joey's suicide, I felt uncomfortable. "Did Larissa ever go to the farmhouse, Ms. Thorne?" the second officer interjected, leaning in closer, his eyes narrowing as if he were trying to read my mind.

The question sent a jolt of anxiety through me. "I... I'm not sure. I mean, I never saw her there," I stammered, my thoughts racing. Why were they focusing on Larissa so much? "Why is she so important?"

PC Harrison nodded, his expression serious. "We're just trying to understand Joey's connections, Ms. Thorne. The more we know about who he was in contact with, the better we can piece together what happened."

I felt my heart rate quicken. "But I barely know her! Why do you think she has anything to do with this?"

"Because, Ms. Thorne," the second officer interjected, "her name keeps coming up in messages leading up to Joey's death. It's not just casual conversation; it seems more significant."

Great. Just great. The walls felt like they were closing in on me. "Look, I can't help you with Larissa. I don't know what her connection to Joey was!" I said, my frustration bubbling to the surface.

They exchanged another glance, and I could see they were trying to put the pieces together. "Do you remember any specific conversations between you and Joey where Larissa might have come up, Ms. Thorne?" PC Harrison asked, his tone shifting to one of genuine curiosity.

I racked my brain, trying to recall any relevant details. "Not really. I mean, we talked about a lot of things. But Larissa? She was just a name. I didn't think anything of it."

"Did you ever see her at any of the gatherings or parties, Ms. Thorne?" the second officer pressed, leaning back slightly, as if gathering his thoughts.

"No! I didn't even know who she was until now!" I said, exasperated. "It's like you're trying to piece together a puzzle that I don't even have the pieces for!"

PC Harrison's expression softened slightly. "We understand this is difficult, Ms. Thorne. We're just trying to get to the bottom of this for Joey's family."

At the mention of Joey's family, the reminder of the gravity of the situation settled heavily in the room. I thought of Maria Hall and how I had only met her twice, but her presence was unforgettable—like a neon sign in a dark alley.

Maria was a woman of graceful resilience, with dark hair streaked with silver, elegantly pulled back into a bun that could probably withstand a hurricane. Her deep-set eyes held a mix of sorrow and strength, framed by delicate lines that seemed to tell stories of laughter, heartache, and perhaps too many late-night soap operas.

"Ms. Thorne, are you ready to proceed?" PC Harrison asked, snapping me back to the present.

"Can we please drop the 'Ms. Thorne' already?" I replied, frustration bubbling beneath the surface. "It's just Dahlia. I'm not a character in a Victorian novel!"

"Fair enough, Ms. Thorne," he said, and for the first time, I detected a hint of empathy in his voice. Perhaps we were all just trying to navigate this complicated web of grief, confusion, and unanswered questions.

"Look," I began, trying to clarify my connection to Larissa. "I only knew her as someone Joey spoke to every now and then. He'd mention her name in passing, but we never really discussed her in detail. It wasn't like they were best friends or anything."

The officers nodded, clearly taking notes. "What kind of things did he say about her, Dahlia?" the second officer asked, leaning forward.

"Honestly, it was mostly small talk," I replied, trying to piece together my memories. "He'd say things like, 'I talked to Larissa today' or 'Larissa sent me a funny meme.' It didn't seem significant at the time. I didn't think much of it."

"Did he ever mention meeting up with her, Dahlia?" PC Harrison inquired, his pen poised over his notepad.

"No, not that I can recall. It was never anything serious," I said, feeling the anxiety creep back in. "I thought it was just a casual acquaintance."

The officers exchanged another look, their brows furrowing in concern. "We really need to dig deeper into this, Dahlia. It's important," the second officer pressed. "Do you have any of those messages on your phone?"

I sighed, knowing this was coming. "I do, but..." I hesitated, glancing at the table where Joey's phone lay. "I recently factory reset the whole thing when I got back from Blackpool. I didn't think I'd need any of those old messages. I just wanted a fresh start."

"Do you remember how long ago that was?" PC Harrison asked, jotting down notes.

"It was just a couple of days ago," I replied, the weight of regret settling in. "I was overwhelmed after everything that happened, and I thought clearing my phone would help. I didn't think about the messages."

The officers exchanged another glance, and I could see their frustration mounting. "So, you don't have any of those conversations saved?" the second officer asked, his tone edged with disappointment.

"No, I'm sorry," I said, my voice barely above a whisper. "I really didn't think it would matter."

"Dahlia, this is crucial," PC Harrison said with an urgency that sent a chill down my spine. "If there was anything in those messages that could provide insight into Joey's state of mind or his relationship with Larissa, it could help us understand what led to his death."

I felt a wave of guilt wash over me. "I really didn't mean to erase anything important. I just wanted to move on from the chaos of it all."

"Understandable, but right now, we're in chaos too," the second officer replied, trying to maintain his composure. "We need to find every scrap of information we can."

I handed my phone over to PC Harrison, feeling a mix of dread and resignation. "I know it's not much, but here it is," I said. "I hope you find something useful, even if it's just the mundane details of my life."

"Thank you, Dahlia," he said, his tone softening slightly. "We appreciate your cooperation. We're just trying to get to the bottom of this, for Joey's family and for you too."

As they began their work, I couldn't shake the feeling that I should have done more. Her name, Larissa, lingered in my mind, a thorny reminder of the secrets still lurking in the shadows of Joey's life. Why had they focused so much on her? With each question hanging in the air, I felt an urgency building within me.

The memory of Larissa lingered like a ghost. The way I had killed her was both exhilarating and haunting, a dance of darkness that played out in my mind like a twisted movie reel. I had felt powerful, in control, as if the world around me had aligned perfectly with my desires.

But then came Joey, stumbling into the scene with that bottle of bleach clutched tightly in his hand. He had never been reckless and that day, his decision felt like a betrayal of the dark world we had created. I remember feeling a mix of horror and disbelief, the bright liquid glistening like a promise of destruction. In an instant, the thrill of Larissa's death evaporated, replaced by a cold dread that seeped into my bones.

Joey's choice shattered something deep within me, something I hadn't even known existed. The exhilaration of power morphed into a chilling sense of loss. I had wanted to embrace the darkness, to revel in it, but now I was left with the weight of guilt and regret. Larissa's death, once a twisted source of pride, felt like a horrific scar etched into my soul. I felt ashamed for the first time in a long time.

I wandered through the forest of my mind, the trees whispering secrets of the past. Each step felt heavy, dragging me deeper into the underworld of my own making. The vibrant colours of the leaves seemed to dull, the world around me fading into shades of grey. The thought twisted and turned, revealing flashes of laughter, of joy, tainted by the shit I had done.

As I stumbled upon a clearing in my mind, I saw her—Larissa. Her laughter echoed in the air, a haunting melody that wrapped around my mind. I reached out, desperate to grasp the remnants of that fleeting moment, but she vanished like smoke in the wind. In her place stood Joey, his eyes hollow, reflecting the emptiness that now resided within me.

"Why?" I whispered, my voice cracking like fragile glass. The question hung in the air, heavy with the weight of unspoken grief. Joey's silence was deafening, a reminder of the choices that had led us here. The thrill of power had turned into a burden, a chain that bound me to memories I could never escape.

I snap out of my mind with a start, the remnants of the thought clinging to me like a cold sweat. The sun streamed through the window, creating the room in a warm light, but it did nothing to chase away the shadows that clung to my heart. The thought felt so real, yet I knew it was just my brain being mixed up.

But the truth lingered—Larissa was gone, and so was the part of me that had revelled in darkness. What remained was a hollow shell, forever changed by the choices I had made and the consequences I had never anticipated.

"Dahlia!" PC Harrison shouted, his voice cutting through the fog of my thoughts like a knife. My heart raced as I snapped back to reality, the weight of my memories crashing down on me like a tidal wave. I looked up, meeting his intense stare, and I felt exposed, as if he could see every dark corner of my mind.

"I… I'm sorry," I stammered, the words spilling out of my mouth like a desperate confession. "I'm just in such a state of shock over Joey." The admission felt like a betrayal of my own emotions, but it was the only truth I could cling to in that moment.

PC Harrison's eyes narrowed, and he side-eyed the other officer in the room, a younger man whose name I couldn't remember. The unspoken tension between them was palpable, and I could feel the weight of suspicion settling over me like a thick fog. In that instant, I felt like prime suspect number one, the spotlight of their scrutiny shining directly on me.

"Shock, huh?" Harrison said, his tone skeptical. "You've been awfully upbeat since we found Joey. Most people would be more... distressed." His words hung in the air, heavy with implications. I could see the gears turning in his mind, questioning my every reaction, every twitch of my body.

My stomach sank. I could sense the doubt swirling around me, the way they whispered among themselves, piecing together a narrative that painted me in a darker light. The thrill I had once felt now morphed into a desperate need to defend myself, to prove that I wasn't the monster they might believe me to be.

The room felt like it was closing in around me, the air heavy with unspoken accusations. PC Harrison leaned closer, his expression a mix of concern and determination. "Dahlia, I need you to understand something. We're not here to vilify you, but we need to know why a man might take his own life in such a brutal manner. It doesn't add up."

His voice softened slightly, but the weight of his words was undeniable. "We'll be searching your phone for any messages or calls that might shed light on this. But for now, I have to place you under arrest for perverting the course of justice."

As he recited the familiar lines, my world shattered into a million pieces. I had seen enough police dramas to know what this meant, but watching it unfold in real life was a different beast entirely. The thought of being handcuffed, of being taken away, made my stomach tighten in a way that felt almost physical.

"Perverting the course of justice?" I echoed, disbelief staining my voice. "What do you think I've done?" My heart pounded in my chest, and I could feel the heat rising in my cheeks. Desperation clawed at me; I needed to defend myself. "I didn't do anything! For fuck sake!'

Harrison's gaze remained steady, but I could sense the shift in the room he could sense my anger. The younger officer, still lingering by the door, shot me a look that felt like a mixture of pity and suspicion. It was as if they had already decided my fate, and I was merely a pawn in their investigation.

"Dahlia," Harrison said, his voice firm but not unkind. "We know things aren't always as they seem. But right now, your story doesn't hold up. We need to figure out why Joey felt he had no other choice."

The implications of his words sank in like a stone. What did they know? What had they pieced together from my life, my interactions? I felt my defences crumbling as the reality of my situation hit me. My mind raced, but my thoughts were tangled in a web of confusion and fear.

"Is that why you think I'm involved?" I asked, my voice barely above a whisper. "Because I cared about him?"

Harrison sighed, rubbing his temples as if trying to ease a headache. "Caring about someone doesn't make you a suspect, Dahlia. But the circumstances surrounding his death raise questions we can't ignore. We have to look at everyone connected to him."

As the gravity of his words settled over me, I felt like I was drowning in uncertainty. My memories of Joey, the laughter we shared, and the moments that defined our friendship began to blur, overshadowed by the looming spectre of suspicion. How had I gone from a concerned friend to a person of interest?

"I swear I didn't hurt him," I pleaded, my voice breaking. "You have to believe me!"

But as the handcuffs clicked around my wrists, I knew that my protests were just whispers lost in the storm of doubt. My heart ached with the weight of their scrutiny, and I felt utterly alone.

The hours dragged on, each tick of the clock a relentless reminder of my growing desperation. I sat in the cold, sterile interrogation room, the fluorescent lights buzzing above like angry wasps, creating an atmosphere thick with tension. The walls, painted a dull grey, seemed to close in on me as I fidgeted in the uncomfortable metal chair, my palms clammy against my jeans. Harrison and Officer Mitchell, who I'd come to know all too well, took turns firing questions at me, their faces a study in stoicism, but I could sense the impatience simmering just beneath their composed exteriors.

"Why did you ignore our calls?" Harrison pressed, his voice steady, but the edge of frustration was unmistakable. "You had multiple missed calls from us. Why didn't you respond?"

I swallowed hard, staring at the table as if it held the answers I so desperately needed. "I… I needed space," I stammered, memories of that harrowing day flooding my mind like a tidal wave. "Everything with Joey's death was too much. I was overwhelmed."

"Overwhelmed enough to reset your phone?" Mitchell interjected, leaning forward, his piercing gaze boring into me. "What were you trying to hide?"

A surge of frustration welled up within me, hot and angry. "I wasn't trying to hide anything! I just wanted a fresh start. I went to Blackpool to get away from everything–" My voice faltered, and I swallowed hard, forcing back tears. "I couldn't bear being in the same place where he… where he died."

The silence that followed felt like an eternity, their eyes boring into me, dissecting my every flinch and breath. I could sense their skepticism, a heavy weight pressing down on my chest, deepening my sense of isolation. It was as if I was trapped in a glass box, my vulnerability on display for them to scrutinise.

"Tell us more about Larissa," Harrison said, shifting his approach, his tone almost casual but with an underlying urgency. "Who is she to you?"

"Joey's girlfriend," I replied, my voice tight, memories of their tumultuous relationship swirling in my mind. "She… she wasn't good to him. She cheated on him with other guys while they were together. He was heartbroken, and before… before he died, he came to me."

"What do you mean by 'came to you'?" Mitchell's tone sharpened, and I could sense the trap closing around me, the noose tightening.

I took a deep breath, feeling exposed, raw, as if my soul was laid bare before them. "We had sex," I admitted, my cheeks burning with shame. "He needed comfort, and I… I wanted to be there for him." The confession hung heavy in the air, a palpable tension that seemed to vibrate with unspoken accusations.

"Why did it take you so long to mention this?" Harrison's eyes narrowed, like a predator searching for cracks in my carefully constructed façade.

"Because it felt wrong," I replied, my voice trembling, the weight of guilt and shame crashing over me like a wave. "I didn't want to complicate things further. I didn't want anyone to think I had anything to do with his death."

"Ms. Thorne," Harrison said, reverting back to the formal address that grated on my nerves. "Your relationship with Joey and your actions afterward raise serious concerns. We need to find Larissa. She might have information that could help us understand what happened."

As they continued to press me, I felt my anger bubbling beneath the surface, a primal instinct to fight back against their relentless questioning. "I haven't done anything wrong! You can't keep treating me like a suspect!" I yelled, my voice echoing off the walls, a desperate plea for them to see the truth of my innocence.

They exchanged glances, and I knew they were weighing their options, deciding how best to manipulate the narrative they were building around me. After what felt like an eternity, they announced that my phone would be sent to a specialised team to recover any deleted data. My heart sank at the thought of them uncovering everything–the incriminating texts, the memories I'd tried to erase, the last desperate messages from Joey that now felt like a noose tightening around my neck.

"If you think of anything else, tell us now, you may need to think of getting yourself a solicitor" Harrison said, his tone almost sympathetic, but I could hear the underlying challenge.

"I don't need a solicitor," I insisted, shaking my head vigorously, the words tumbling out in a rush. "I haven't done anything wrong." But doubt crept in, gnawing at my insides like a hungry beast. What if they found something that painted me in a different light, something that twisted the truth beyond recognition?

Eventually, they decided to bail me pending further investigation. As I walked out of that room, a mixture of relief and anger coursed through me, a chaotic storm of emotions. I was free, but the weight of their scrutiny lingered like a shadow, a constant reminder of the storm brewing just beneath the surface.

As I stepped into the cool air outside, the weight of the world pressed down on me. I felt a gnawing fear in my gut–what if they discovered the blood lust I had to Jessica, Leah, and Larissa? The thought haunted me, twisting my stomach in knots. I was caught in a web of my own making, each thread pulling tighter, suffocating me. I couldn't shake the feeling that the worst was yet to come. The world felt like it was spiralling out of control, and I was powerless to stop it. Days turned into weeks, each one dragging by like a snail on a leisurely stroll. I found myself staring at my phone, willing it to ring, hoping for some news—any news—from the police, but it remained as silent as a tomb. The silence was deafening, an echoing reminder of my isolation that had me questioning my sanity. I spent countless nights tossing and turning, haunted by memories of Joey and the choices I had made. Honestly, even my dreams were turning into melodramatic soap operas.

In a desperate bid to escape the suffocating atmosphere of my own home, I decided to seek out my brother Ren. Our parents had always had a penchant for flower names—my mother was named Iris, and my father, the ever-so-god-awful name of Derek, his parents celled had opted for something a little less poetic. But somehow, our surname, Thorne, seemed to fit perfectly with the floral theme—a delightful juxtaposition of beauty and danger. I hadn't seen Ren in months, but the thought of his familiar face brought a flicker of hope.

I hopped on a bus, the landscape flashing by in a blur of greens and browns, each town and field reminding me of simpler times. After what felt like an eternity, I arrived at Ren's flat, a few towns away. It was a modest building, worn but welcoming, with graffiti art splashed across the walls that looked like the rebellious offspring of a paint can and a wall. As I climbed the creaky stairs to the second floor, I could hear the distant sounds of laughter and video game sound effects wafting through the hallway, accompanied by the unmistakable scent of microwaved ramen.

Ren shared the flat with a few friends, all of whom were as different as they were inseparable—a motley crew that embodied the essence of a stereotypical gamer household. The door swung open, revealing a typical gamer scene. The living room was cluttered with half-empty energy drink cans, more pizza boxes than I could count, and an assortment of gaming consoles that looked like they were auditioning for an antique roadshow. The coffee table, covered in a blanket that had definitely seen better days, was home to a pile of controllers and snacks, as if it were a shrine to the gods of gaming.

"Ren!" I called, my voice cutting through the cacophony of sounds. He emerged from a dimly lit hallway, his face lighting up like a kid in a candy store.

"Dahlia! What are you doing here?" he exclaimed, enveloping me in a bear hug that lifted me off my feet. I swear, I heard a few bones crack, but it was worth it for the warmth of his embrace.

"I needed a break. Can I crash here for a bit?" I asked, my voice tinged with weariness.

"Of course! Just try not to trip over the mess. We've been busy with the new game release," he replied, stepping aside to let me in.

As I stepped inside, I took in the scene. To my left, a lanky guy with messy hair and a beanie sat cross-legged on the floor, fingers flying over the keyboard of a gaming laptop. That was Zack, a tech wizard who could build a gaming rig from scratch and had a penchant for conspiracy theories. I once overheard him arguing with Ren about whether Bigfoot was actually a government experiment gone wrong. To my right, perched on the edge of the couch, was Amy, a fierce competitor in online tournaments.

She was decked out in a graphic tee featuring a legendary fantasy character and was animatedly discussing strategies with Ren, her passion rivalling that of a sports commentator during the American Super Bowl.

"I'm glad you came," Ren said, guiding me into the living room. "We could use more chaos around here—Zack's starting to think he's the next Einstein or something."

The flat itself was a blend of mismatched furniture—a sofa that looked like it had survived a war, a coffee table with enough chips to start a poker game, and beanbags strewn about like the aftermath of a pillow fight gone wrong. Posters of iconic video games adorned the walls, each one telling a story of late-night battles, epic wins, and defeats that had become legendary among their friends.

As I settled onto one of the beanbags, I felt a wave of comfort wash over me, interrupted only by the sound of Ren tripping over a pizza box as he tried to grab a soda. "Watch out! It's a dangerous world out here!" he joked, flashing me a sheepish grin.

I shared snippets of what had been happening, my voice trembling as I recounted my time in the interrogation room, the weight of suspicion hanging over me like a dark cloud. The gang listened intently, their expressions a mix of concern and disbelief.

"Don't worry about them," Ren said, placing a reassuring hand on my shoulder. "You'll get through this. We're here for you. Plus, if anyone comes knocking, we can always distract them with the latest gaming lore. No one can resist a good 'Who's stronger: Batman or Wolverine?' debate."

As the days turned into a blur of gaming marathons, late-night snacks, and laughter, I found a temporary reprieve from my anxiety. It was a distraction I desperately needed, but the shadows of my past still loomed, lurking just beyond the fringes of my newfound solace. I couldn't shake the feeling that the police might come knocking again, and I was terrified of what they might uncover. But for now, at least, I was surrounded by family, friends, and the comforting chaos of Ren's flat—a small sanctuary in the midst of my storm, complete with a side of absurdity and a sprinkle of laughter.

Me and Ren start a conversation about our names.

"And let's not forget Daisy, our beloved cat, who had ruled our household like a furry dictator" Ren laughs.

I half-expected to see her lounging somewhere in the flat, but alas, she was long gone, probably off chasing imaginary butterflies in the afterlife. The memory of her antics brought a smile to my face—even in the chaos, there was always room for a little nostalgia.

The next morning, I was jolted awake by the tantalising aroma of something delicious wafting through the air. I squinted against the bright sunlight streaming through the window, momentarily disoriented before the realisation struck me: Ren was making breakfast. A smile crept across my face as I pulled myself up, feeling a warm wave of comfort wash over me. My brother had undergone such a remarkable transformation. The mischievous kid I remembered had grown into the perfect older brother—thoughtful and attentive—especially considering how he once set off the fire alarm while attempting to make toast.

"Breakfast in bed, just like you've always dreamed!" he called out, entering the room with a tray piled high with fluffy pancakes, syrup, and what appeared to be an astonishing amount of whipped cream. "I even managed not to set off the fire alarm this time!"

"Wow, I'm genuinely impressed," I replied, a chuckle escaping my lips as I accepted the tray from him. "What's the occasion? Did you win the lottery overnight or something?"

"Just thought you could use a little TLC," he said, plopping down on the edge of the bed with a grin. "We've been through a lot, and I'm not letting you starve while you're here."

As I dug into the pancakes, savouring the sweetness of the syrup, my moment of bliss was abruptly interrupted by my new mobile phone buzzing insistently on the bedside table. It was a cheap model, one I had picked up recently to stay in touch with my work colleagues while I was out of a job due to everything that had been happening—and, of course, to keep in contact with the investigation team, to whom I had reluctantly given my number.

I glanced at the screen, my stomach dropping as I saw the caller ID: PC Harrison. "Oh no," I muttered, my appetite evaporating in an instant.

"Who is it?" Ren asked, concern flickering across his face.

"It's the police," I replied, my voice shaky as I answered the call. "Harrison wants me to come to the station immediately."

The words hit me like a punch to the gut, and suddenly, the room began to spin. I couldn't help but feel a wave of nausea wash over me. "What if they've uncovered something? What if they think I'm guilty?" I whispered, panic creeping into my voice.

Ren's expression softened as he leaned closer, wrapping an arm around my shoulders. "Hey, hey, it's going to be okay. You're not guilty of anything. Just remember that."

"I love you, Ren," I said, my voice trembling. "I hope you'll visit me in prison."

He let out a hearty laugh that reverberated in the room, easing some of my tension. "You'll be just fine, little wildflower. You're tougher than you think."

"Easy for you to say," I shot back, rolling my eyes but feeling a bit lighter. "You're not the one about to face another round of interrogation."

"Let me drive you down there," he insisted, a determined look gleaming in his eyes. "And I'll stay with you as long as I can upload my YouTube videos from your house."

"Right, because that's the priority," I said, a small smirk creeping onto my face. "Gotta keep the subscribers entertained."

"Exactly." He sprang up and began to pack his Xbox, tossing in a few games as if preparing for an epic road trip. "If I can stream while you're chatting with the cops, I'll be the most popular gamer in the country."

I couldn't help but laugh at his antics, the absurdity of the situation momentarily distracting me from the dread pooling in my stomach. Ren had always had a knack for lightening the mood, even in the bleakest of times.

"Just don't play anything too loud while I'm in there, okay?" I said, standing up and nervously pushing my hair back.

"Promise! I'll keep it nice and chill for you," he assured me, his tone playful yet sincere.

As I prepared to leave, I couldn't shake the feeling of impending doom that loomed over me, but Ren's unwavering support grounded me. Together, we headed out into the crisp morning air, and I clutched my phone tightly, feeling a mix of dread and determination. Whatever awaited me at the police station, I knew I wouldn't be facing it alone.

As we settled into the car, the familiar scent of Ren's old air freshener—something that smelled vaguely like a combination of pine trees and desperation—washed over me. He cranked up the radio, blasting a mix of nostalgic tunes that transported me back to simpler times, like summer afternoons spent at our parents' farmhouse, where life had felt carefree.

"Remember the time we tried to build that treehouse?" Ren chuckled, his eyes glinting with mischief. "You insisted we could do it all by ourselves, and then we ended up with a glorified wooden box that fell apart the second we climbed in?"

"Oh, please," I replied, rolling my eyes. "I was ten! And you were the one who brought the power tools without reading the instructions."

"Hey, I still stand by my decision to use the chainsaw," he said, grinning. "That treehouse was a masterpiece of engineering."

I tried to change the subject quickly, my stomach twisting at the memories. "So, uh, how's your YouTube channel doing?" I asked, hoping to steer him away from the farmhouse and all the memories it held, especially the ones that were too painful to revisit.

Ren glanced over, his expression shifting to one of concern. "What's really been happening, Dahlia? You can talk to me, you know."

I felt a lump form in my throat. I couldn't bear to explain everything to him; he wouldn't understand, not really. He had his own way of seeing the world, one that often left little room for the messiness of emotions and the chaos I was embroiled in. "It's just… Joey had a bit of an accident at the farmhouse," I blurted out, opting for the half-truth. "The police are worried it might be connected to me since I'm always there."

Ren looked puzzled, his brow furrowing. "What kind of accident?"

"Uh, he hurt himself. Nothing serious, just a scrape or something," I lied, feeling the guilt gnaw at me. "And the police are worried, you know, because they think I might have something to do with it."

His response was characteristically simple. "Okay." Just like that, he accepted it, his typical autistic way of processing things shining through. There was a strange comfort in his straightforwardness, but it also made my heart ache for the truth I couldn't share.

We drove on in silence, the weight of unspoken words hanging between us. As we neared the police station, I felt a wave of dread wash over me. "Hey, why don't you grab yourself a McDonald's or something?" I suggested, trying to lighten the mood. "You can have a Big Mac while I'm being interrogated. It'll be like a mini vacation for you."

Ren raised an eyebrow, a smirk playing on his lips. "You think I'd be able to enjoy a burger knowing my sister is possibly going to jail? You underestimate my guilt."

"Let's be real, you'd just be thinking about how you'd have to pick me up on the way out. You know I'll need one of those burgers after this," I said, forcing a weak laugh.

As he parked outside the police station, my heart sank further into my stomach. I didn't want to be in prison just yet. The only reason I felt fear at this moment was that it definitely wasn't my time—this wasn't how my story was meant to end. I had unfinished business, a lingering darkness that needed to be addressed before I could even consider such a fate.

Taking a deep breath, I stepped out of the car, the familiar doors of the police station looming ahead. Each step felt heavier, as if the very ground was trying to pull me back, to keep me away from the inevitable confrontation inside. I glanced over at Ren, who gave me an encouraging nod, a small gesture that somehow made all the difference in that moment.

As I walked through those overly familiar doors, a wave of nausea hit me. If this was my end, I only felt partially satisfied with the path I'd taken. The deaths I had caused, the choices I had made—they lingered like ghosts, shadows that danced just out of reach. I wasn't ready to face the consequences, but here I was, teetering on the precipice of a dark abyss, my heart pounding with the weight of everything I had yet to say, yet to confront.

And in that moment, I had to wonder—was this truly my ending, or just another chapter in a story that refused to continue to be written?

As I pushed through the police station doors, they creaked ominously, sounding like an ancient haunted house beckoning me to step inside. A familiar sense of dread washed over me, mingling with the stale scent of day-old coffee and the pungent aroma of regret that seemed to cling to the walls like an unwanted guest who just wouldn't leave. The fluorescent lights buzzed overhead, flickering like they were trying to signal an emergency that only I could sense. I really hoped someone would get around to changing that bulb, as it cast an unflattering glow on everything—especially my own reflection in the overly polished surfaces. Honestly, the lighting made it look like the station was run by a group of humans with OCD; my mother would have adored the cleanliness but found the ambiance utterly joyless.

As I approached the custody officer I had seen before, I couldn't help but notice how she sat behind a plastic barrier, like an exotic animal on display at a zoo. And despite the gravity of the situation, I found myself thinking she was incredibly attractive.

For a brief moment, my mind wandered down an inappropriate path, picturing her without her uniform. I quickly shook off the thought, chiding myself for letting my imagination run wild in a place where people were likely discussing the finer points of criminal law—or worse, their favourite flavours of instant coffee.

"Hi, Ms. Thorne," she greeted me, her voice smooth and confident, cutting through the haze of my wandering thoughts like a warm knife through cold butter. "PC Harrison isn't here today, but another officer, PC Whitley, will come out shortly to have a chat with you."

"Thanks," I replied, forcing a casual tone despite the fluttering anxiety in my stomach that felt like a small bird trying to escape. I took a seat in the waiting area, which had all the charm of an abandoned dentist's office—complete with the awkward silence and the faint smell of antiseptic—trying to appear composed while my mind raced with endless possibilities about what would happen next.

Just when I thought I might dissolve into a puddle of nerves right there on the floor, PC Whitley emerged from the back. He was a middle-aged man with kind eyes and a slightly worn face that suggested he had seen his fair share of life's heavier burdens—like a father who had just discovered his teenage daughter's TikTok account. Seriously, where had he been this whole time? He approached me with a calm demeanour, and his presence felt oddly soothing amidst the chaos of my thoughts.

"Good morning, Ms. Thorne," he said, extending a hand. "I'm PC Whitley. I understand you've had quite the ordeal."

"Yeah, you could say that," I replied, shaking his hand. A boring type of adrenaline coursed through me as we conversed normally, but it felt surreal, as if I were in a bizarre dream where everyone spoke in monotone and the world was slightly askew—like a funhouse mirror version of reality.

"We've been reviewing your case," he continued, his tone professional yet gentle. "I wanted to let you know that all charges have been dropped. The County Court saw no wrongdoing on your end due to a lack of evidence."

Relief washed over me like a refreshing wave at the beach, tension releasing from my shoulders like a deflating balloon. But as he handed back my old phone, I noticed a concerned look on his face that made my stomach churn again, like I had swallowed a rock the size of a grapefruit.

"However," he said, his voice lowering slightly as if he were sharing a state secret, "if you hear from Larissa, please inform the police immediately. Her family wants closure."

Another wave of nausea hit me at the mention of Larissa. I nodded, swallowing hard as I processed the weight of his words. "Of course," I replied, my voice barely above a whisper, the knot in my stomach tightening uncomfortably.

PC Whitley concluded the conversation with a reassuring smile that felt like a warm blanket on a cold night. "You're free to leave, but please keep in contact."

I nodded, gratitude and relief flooding me, but I couldn't get out of that place fast enough. I practically bolted for the exit, pushing through the doors like a contestant on a game show racing for the grand prize, stepping back into the fresh air outside. The sensation of freedom was intoxicating, and the sun felt warmer on my skin, as if the universe was giving me a congratulatory high-five.

I quickly made my way around to McDonald's, a familiar beacon of comfort that promised greasy fries and a moment of normalcy. The air was fresher than ever, and I could hardly wait to embrace Ren. He had been my rock through all of this the last few days and I longed to see his face, to share the relief that coursed through me now that I was no longer facing charges.

As I approached the fast-food joint, I spotted Ren waiting outside, pacing anxiously like he was waiting for a bus that would never arrive. When our eyes met, his face broke into a wide grin, and I felt an overwhelming sense of gratitude.

"Get me a Big Mac!" I smile wildly.

Gnomes, Giggles And Secrets

THIRTEEN

Days passed since that fateful call to Bella, each one stretching out like a rubber band ready to snap. The anticipation hung in the air, thick and tantalising, as I counted down the hours until our reunion. I found myself daydreaming about the evening we had planned—an escape from the ordinary into the embrace of the familiar, yet somehow thrillingly unpredictable.

Every morning, I awoke with Bella's laughter echoing in my mind, a sweet melody that chased away the lingering shadows of my past. I busied myself with preparations, cleaning up the farm and ensuring everything was in order. Each chore felt electrified, a chance to transform my mundane surroundings into a backdrop for whatever mischief we might conjure up.

I even considered how I could playfully embellish our time together. Perhaps I could set up a scavenger hunt around the farm, hiding small treasures that would lead her through fields and pastures. The idea of her racing against the clock, her laughter ringing out as she pieced together the clues, sent a thrill down my spine. It was a small way to inject adrenaline into our time together, a reminder that life could still be full of surprises.

As the days rolled on, I felt a strange mixture of excitement and anxiety. I kept recalling the darker thoughts that had lingered in the back of my mind, the shadows that had once consumed me. But Bella's presence felt like a light cutting through the darkness, illuminating paths I thought were long forgotten.

The night before she was due to arrive, I lay awake, staring at the ceiling, my mind racing with possibilities. What if she didn't enjoy herself? What if my attempts at fun fell flat? I shook my head, banishing those thoughts like ghosts.

Finally, the day arrived. The sun rose bright and by the time the afternoon rolled around, I was practically buzzing with energy. I threw on a casual shirt and jeans, determined to look effortlessly cool. I checked my watch, counting down the minutes until Bella would arrive.

When the sound of her car engine finally broke the quiet, my heart raced. I dashed outside, the anticipation swirling within me like a summer storm. As her car pulled up, I felt that familiar rush of adrenaline, a mixture of excitement and nerves coursing through my veins.

The moment she stepped out of the car, all my worries melted away. Bella was radiant, her hair catching the sunlight and her smile lighting up the space around her. "Hey there!" she called out, her voice bright and welcoming.

"Hey! You made it!" I grinned, unable to hide my enthusiasm.

"Wouldn't miss it for the world," she replied, bounding toward me. We embraced, and in that moment, I felt the weight of the last few days lift off my shoulders.

As we pulled back, I could see the curiosity gleaming in her eyes. "So, what's the plan for today?"

I couldn't help but chuckle. "Oh, just a little adventure I've cooked up. Are you ready for some fun?"

"Always," she said, her grin infectious.

And with that, I led her into the heart of the farm, ready to unleash a whirlwind of excitement and unexpected twists. The adrenaline was already surging, and I knew this evening would be anything but ordinary. The shadows of my past faded into the backdrop as we stepped into the light, ready to create new memories—wonderfully twisted and full of surprises.

As Bella stepped into my home, the familiar warmth of the space enveloped us, but there was an underlying chill that seemed to accompany the shadows lurking in the corners. The walls were adorned with quirky photographs and a few odd pieces of art I had collected over the years—an unusual mix of the whimsical and the macabre. It was a reflection of my mind, a blend of light and dark, and it seemed to intrigue her.

"Wow, you've got quite the collection here!" she exclaimed, glancing around my bedroom. Her eyes sparkled with curiosity, but I could sense an edge of mischief.

"Yeah, I've always been a bit of a scribbler," I admitted, trying to maintain my composure. A flush crept up my neck as I realised the notebooks scattered about were a treasure trove of my inner workings—thoughts, sketches, and ramblings that ranged from the absurd to the downright sinister. Part of me secretly wished she would read them, while another part screamed in horror at the thought of her discovering my more twisted musings.

She picked up a notebook with a tattered cover, flipping it open to reveal a jumble of handwritten notes and bizarre doodles. "What's this one about?"

"Oh, you know, just the usual—existential dread, the occasional plot for world domination," I replied with a smirk, trying to keep things light while my heart raced.

Bella raised an eyebrow, her curiosity piqued. "World domination? Now you've got my attention."

"Sure," I said, leaning in conspiratorially. "But only if you promise to be my right-hand woman. We'll rule the world with a blend of chaos and charm. And snacks, of course."

She laughed, flipping through the pages, her expression shifting as she came across a particularly dark sketch—a creature with twisted limbs and a sinister grin. "What on earth is this? A demon from your nightmares?"

"Actually, that's just my attempt at drawing my ex," I quipped, trying to mask the truth with humour. "She was a real piece of work."

Bella giggled, and I could feel the tension ease slightly, even as I watched her read on, my heart pounding. Each turn of the page felt like a gamble. Would she find the darker entries—the scribbled thoughts on despair and the absurdity of life? The little snippets about my fascination with the bizarre and the grotesque?

"Look at this!" she exclaimed, pointing to a doodle of a skull wearing a party hat. "This is amazing! A celebration of mortality? Dark, but I love it!"

"Thank you! I call it 'The Grim Reaper's Birthday Bash.' It was a wild party until he showed up," I replied, grinning. "You know, he really knows how to kill the vibe."

"Very punny," she said, rolling her eyes playfully but with a smile. "But seriously, you should consider showcasing this stuff. It's both hilarious and… well, slightly terrifying."

I chuckled, feeling a surge of warmth at her encouragement. "Maybe I'll throw an art show called 'The Dark Side of the Moon' and serve snacks shaped like various organs. It'll be a hit."

Bella laughed, but there was a moment of silence as she flipped to a page filled with more raw thoughts, the ink darker and more frantic. "What's this?" she asked, her voice dropping to a whisper as she read a line that hinted at my struggles with anxiety.

"It's, um, just a little existential crisis I had one night," I replied, trying to shrug it off. "Nothing to worry about. Just me contemplating the futility of existence, you know, the usual."

She looked up at me, her expression serious for a moment. "You know, it's okay to feel that way. It's like you're wrestling with your own shadows. And trust me, we all have them, even if we pretend otherwise."

I nodded, feeling a mixture of relief and vulnerability. "I guess I just find comfort in the darkness sometimes. It's like a twisted friend that keeps me company."

"Twisted friends are the best kind," she said with a wink, flipping the page again. "But you should let the light in too. Balance, right?"

"Balance, yes. Like a tightrope walker over a pit of ravenous alligators. It's all about the thrill," I replied, my voice dripping with sarcasm.

"Exactly! And if you fall, at least you'll go down in a blaze of glory," she said, laughing again, and I felt a surge of affection for her.

As she continued to browse through my notebooks, I couldn't shake the feeling of excitement mixed with trepidation. What if she discovered the darker parts of me that I had kept hidden? But as we shared laughter and banter, I realised that perhaps I was ready to let her in—into the chaos, the mystery, and the delightful darkness that was me.

And just as I was about to suggest we embark on a scavenger hunt of my own creation, I noticed her eyes widen at an entry that detailed an absurd plan for a heist involving rubber chickens and glitter bombs. "Oh, this is brilliant! You've got to show me how to pull this off," she said, her enthusiasm infectious.

"Only if you promise to wear a mask. I hear it adds to the mystery," I replied, a wicked grin spreading across my face.

With Bella by my side, I felt a sense of adventure bubbling up within me. Together, we could embrace the darkness, the humour, and the mystery. And who knew what kinds of trouble we might stir up in the process?

As Bella continued to flip through my notebooks, I could feel the tension building in the air—a mixture of excitement and the looming dread of what she might discover. I watched as her fingers hovered over a particular notebook, the one that contained my thoughts about Jessica and the aftermath of her death. The memory of that time was like a dark cloud hanging over me, and I desperately hoped she wouldn't delve too deep.

She paused, her brow furrowing slightly as she picked it up, the cover faded and worn. "What's this one about?" she asked, her curiosity evident. I could see the gears turning in her mind, and I knew I had to act fast.

"Uh, you know," I said, trying to sound casual, "it's just some really boring stuff. You wouldn't want to read it. It's mostly about my theories on the mating rituals of garden gnomes." I flashed her a grin, hoping to deflect her interest.

Bella raised an eyebrow, clearly intrigued but not entirely convinced. "Garden gnomes? Now that's a topic I didn't expect. Enlighten me!"

"Right! So, I was thinking that they must have some elaborate social structure, possibly involving secret gnome meetings and a hierarchy based on how many mushrooms they can balance on their heads," I said, my voice bubbling with mock seriousness.

She laughed, shaking her head. "Only you would come up with something so ridiculous. But I have to admit, I'm kind of curious about the gnome politics now!"

"Ah, yes, you see, they're quite cutthroat. It's a real turf war out there in the flowerbeds," I said, trying to keep the momentum going. I could feel her interest shift, and it filled me with relief.

But just as I thought I had successfully distracted her, I remembered the post-it notes—those remnants of a darker time that had once cluttered my parents' house, now nestled within that very notebook, remnants of my grief and confusion. I took a deep breath, mentally reminding myself to remain composed.

"Speaking of curious topics," I said, seizing the moment, "let's talk about something a bit more... personal. What's your take on the whole idea of relationships and sex?"

Bella's eyes widened slightly, a mixture of surprise and intrigue flashing across her face. "Wow, that's a shift!" she said, her cheeks flushing a delicate shade of pink. "But, okay, I'm game. What do you want to know?"

I grinned, delighted by the way I had thrown her off balance. "Just curious about your thoughts. Is it overrated or the best thing ever? And, you know, do garden gnomes have a say in it?"

She laughed, momentarily caught off guard. "Well, I think sex can be great, but it really depends on the connection you have with the person. And as for gnomes? I'd say they're probably more interested in their mushroom conquests than anything else!"

"Ha! See? Now we're back on the right track," I said, relieved that the conversation had taken a light-hearted turn. "But seriously, do you think it's one of those things that gets better with practice, like cooking or knitting, or is it just one of those things you either have or you don't?"

Bella considered this for a moment, her expression thoughtful. "I think it's definitely something that can be improved with practice. It's like, you know, learning to ride a bike. You fall a few times but eventually, you get the hang of it. Or, you could just end up in a world of awkwardness."

"Awkwardness is my middle name," I shot back, chuckling at the absurdity of it all. "But I like the bike analogy. Maybe we should start a club–'The Awkward Riders'–and have weekly meetings to discuss all things uncomfortable."

"Count me in!" she replied, laughter spilling from her lips. The tension that had filled the room moments before evaporated, replaced by an easy camaraderie that made my heart swell.

As we bantered back and forth, I could see the way her eyes sparkled with mischief and joy, and I felt a sense of relief wash over me. The notebook about Jessica remained untouched for now, the darkness momentarily pushed aside, replaced by the lightness of our conversation. Bella's presence was like a cool breeze, bringing with it the scent of sweet vanilla and the promise of a summer storm. She had perched herself mischievously on the edge of my bed, her red hair cascading down her bare shoulders, framing her emerald eyes. She was dressed in a simple white tank top and cut-off shorts, the fabric hugging her curves in a way that left very little to the imagination. Her legs were crossed, and the way her foot bobbed up and down revealed a hint of nervousness or perhaps excitement.

Her body was a canvas of ink, with tattoos snaking up her arms and across her ribcage. They told a story of her life, a silent autobiography etched into her skin. Each design was intricate and mesmerising, drawing my gaze like a map of hidden desires and secret adventures. Her sweet voice was a siren's song, luring me in, and my mind was already racing with the days of passion that lay ahead.

The anticipation was thick in the air, a palpable force that seemed to charge every interaction. We had flirted and danced around the subject, but now, with her so close and the heat of the day pressing down on us, the conversation naturally veered towards sex. Her eyes sparkled with mischief as she spoke, and I knew she was eager to explore the depths of our desires together. I took a deep breath, trying to compose myself, knowing that I needed to play it cool, not wanting to scare her off with the intensity of what I had in mind. But the truth was, the days of waiting had honed my hunger for her into a razor-sharp need.

A gentle breeze danced through the open window, carrying with it the scent of rain-soaked earth from outside. Bella lay on the bed, her body a canvas of freckles scattered across pale inked skin, her chest rising and falling with each deep breath.

Her eyes fluttered open to meet mine, a lazy smile playing on her lips. I watched as she stretched out her hand, beckoning me closer with a twirl of her finger. The mattress dipped under my weight as I approached, the warmth of her body seeping into mine as we touched.

Her hair, a fiery cascade of red, spilled across the pillow like a waterfall of embers. I gently gathered it in my hand, lifting it off her neck to expose the smoothness of her skin. She shivered slightly at my touch, a silent invitation for more. My other hand traced the curve of her shoulder, down the side of her breast, and along her ribcage until it rested on her hip.

Our eyes locked, and she tilted her head back, offering her neck to me. I leaned in, pressing my lips to her pulse point, feeling the rapid beat of her heart. She sighed contentedly, her hand finding its way to the back of my neck to pull me closer. The heat between us grew, a tangible force that seemed to thicken the very air in the room.

"Dahlia," Bella murmured, her breath hot against my neck, "are you sure you don't mind?" Her words were a tease, a challenge, wrapped in a tone that made it clear she knew damn well I didn't mind. In fact, the anticipation was making me wetter.

My hand slid down her body, tracing the curve of her waist to the jut of her hip, "I don't mind, Bella," I said, my voice low and filled with the promise of what was to come.

"But if you keep talking, I might not be able to hold back much longer."

The phone on the nightstand buzzed to life, a jarring intrusion to the thick sexual tension that had settled in the air. Bella groaned, a sound that was half annoyance and half arousal, as she reached for the device. "It's my fucking mother," she whispered, rolling her eyes. "Can you imagine?"

The call was a slap to our senses, bringing us back to reality. With a dramatic flounce, she slid out from under me, her body leaving a warm, damp imprint on the bed. She grabbed her discarded shirt, sliding it over her breasts with a sigh. "I have to take this," she said, glancing over her shoulder with a wink. "Don't go anywhere."

As she stepped into the bathroom, I couldn't help but admire the view of her round, bare cheeks, the light from the hallway casting shadows on her pale skin. One of tattoos, a poorly done caricature of a dolphin riding a dick, made me smirk. Bella, always full of surprises it seemed.

The door clicked shut behind her, and I could hear the muffled sounds of her voice as she talked to her mom. I lay there, naked and feeling more exposed than ever, the scent of our desire lingering in the air. The sudden shift from passion to shitty conversation was absurdly amusing.

Bella emerged from the bathroom, fully dressed now, looking at me with a mix of amusement and mischief. She licked her lips, and I knew she was thinking of what we'd just been about to do. "Looks like I've got to go," she said, her voice a playful purr. "But, Dahlia, don't worry, I'll be back for that later."

Her eyes trailed down my body, and she bit her lip before leaning in to whisper in my ear, "I'm going to make you beg for it, darling." With that, she blew me a kiss and slipped out the door, leaving me in a state of heightened arousal and frustration.

The room was eerily quiet without her laughter, without the sound of fabric rustling as she moved. I sat up, the cool air hitting my overheated skin, and took a moment to process the sudden change in plans. Bella had always had a way of leaving me wanting more, but this was a new level of torture.

As I stood to get dressed, the image of her tattoo flashed through my mind, and I couldn't help but chuckle. It was so ridiculous, so her. I knew that when she returned, I'd have to bring it up again, maybe even tease her into a blush. It was a power move, something to keep the upper hand when she was so obviously eager to continue what we'd started.

But for now, I was left to my thoughts, my body still thrumming with need. I couldn't wait for the moment she'd be in my arms again, calling out my name, begging me to make her come. And when she was finally mine, I'd make sure she'd never forget it.

As I paced the living room, anticipation thrummed within me like a tightly wound spring—if I were a cartoon character, I might have been bouncing off the walls like a hyperactive rubber ball. The soft glow of the lamp illuminated my surroundings, casting gentle shadows on the walls, while the lingering scent of her favourite vanilla candle wrapped around me like a warm embrace. A smile tugged at my lips as I thought of her—how her mere presence could transform any space into something vibrant and alive, like a human sunbeam with a penchant for mischief.

To channel my restless energy, I decided to tidy up. I fluffed the cushions on the couch, smoothing out the creases, and collected stray items littering the coffee table. Each movement felt imbued with purpose, as if I were preparing for an Olympic event in couch fluffing. I wanted everything to be perfect for her arrival, a little sanctuary that reflected how much I cared—or at least how much I cared about not getting a sarcastic remark about my housekeeping skills.

Once the room was neat, I found myself drawn to the kitchen, where the memory of our last spontaneous cooking session flitted through my mind. I could still hear her laughter, a sweet melody that filled the air as we playfully tossed flour at each other. It was a scene straight out of a cooking show gone wrong, complete with me wearing a flour-dusted apron that looked suspiciously like a modern art piece. I rummaged through the cabinets, pulling out fresh ingredients for a simple yet heartfelt dinner. Nothing too elaborate, just the culinary equivalent of saying, "I've been waiting for you and I promise I won't burn down the kitchen this time."

As I chopped vegetables, my thoughts drifted back to that tattoo—the vibrant, oversized dragon that coiled around her arm like a fierce guardian. I chuckled at the memory, picturing the mix of pride and slight embarrassment that played across her face whenever I teased her about it. "You know," I'd say, "if you ever need a wingman, I think your dragon is more than qualified."

With the food simmering on the stove, I returned to the living room, sinking into the couch as I curated the perfect playlist. Music had a magical way of setting the mood, and tonight was no exception. I selected a few of our favourite songs, each one a piece of our shared history, eager to weave another memorable evening together. I even considered adding that one ridiculous song we both loved to mock, just for the laughs.

As I waited, I took a moment to reflect on everything we had experienced—those stolen glances, the lingering touches that ignited sparks between us. The thought of her calling out my name, her voice thick with desire, sent shivers racing down my spine. My heart quickened as I imagined the intoxicating heat of her body pressed against mine, the soft gasps that would escape her lips. I could almost hear her laughing, "You really think you can handle all this? You may need a dragon to help you out!"

Suddenly, the sound of knocking at the door jolted me from my reverie, adrenaline surging through my veins. A sly grin spread across my face as I quickly composed myself, striking a pose like a weird sitcom character. This was the moment I had been waiting for. I had to play it cool, just enough to keep the playful tension simmering between us, but not so cool that she thought I was auditioning for a role in a romantic comedy.

As I approach and open the door, I find Bella standing there, looking as if she's just seen a ghost. Her face is pale, and her eyes are wide with fear.

"What's wrong?" I ask, genuinely concerned.

"It's my mum," she says, her voice shaking. "She called me earlier with a headache, and when I rushed down to her, she had passed out. I called an ambulance, and they took her to the hospital. I've been up there all day, but I wanted to come see you before I go back."

"Oh, honey, I'm so sorry to hear that," I say, wrapping her in a tight hug. "I can only imagine how scared you must be."

Bella looks up at me, her eyes filled with tears. "Honestly, I just want to forget about it all for a little while and enjoy some time with you. Can we do that?"

I smile warmly, my heart melting at her request. "Of course, we can. Let's make the most of the time we have together."

Bella's face lights up, and she pulls me towards the bed. "I've been thinking about this all day," she says, her voice low and husky.

"Oh, really?" I say, a mischievous grin spreading across my face. "Do tell."

Bella blushes, but she doesn't look away. "I want to feel you, all of you," she says, her eyes meeting mine.

I don't hesitate, pulling her close and kissing her deeply. We tumble onto the bed, our bodies tangled together as we explore each other. I can feel the heat building between us, the connection we share growing stronger with every touch.

As Bella and I head to the bed we'd left in a state of wanting more earlier, the tension between us is palpable. I can see the longing in her eyes, and I know that she wants me just as much as I want her.

Without a word, I lean in and kiss her, my tongue seeking out hers as our lips meet. She responds eagerly, her hands reaching up to tangle in my hair as we deepen the kiss.

I can feel the heat building between us as we continue to kiss, our bodies pressed close together. I can feel her nipples harden through her shirt, and I can't help but reach up to touch them.

She moans as I caress her breasts, her hands reaching down to undo the buttons of her shirt. I help her, pulling it off and revealing her lacy bra. I can't help but stare at her perfect breasts, and I lean in to take one of her nipples in my mouth, through the lace. She arches her back, moaning as I tease her nipple with my tongue. I can feel her hands reaching down to undo my pants, and I help her, kicking them off and revealing my bare legs.

She pushes me back onto the bed, climbing on top of me and straddling my hips. I can feel her heat, and I know that she's ready for me. She grinds her hips against mine, and I can feel her wetness through her thong. I reach up and undo her bra, freeing her breasts and taking one of her nipples in my mouth. She moans, her hands reaching down to touch herself. I can see her fingers moving beneath her thong and I know that she's close.

I reach down and slip off her underwear, revealing her wet and ready pussy. I can't help but stare at it, and I lean in to taste her. She moans as I lick her clit, her hands reaching down to hold my head in place. I continue to lick and tease her, my tongue working in circles around her clit. She's moaning and writhing, her body begging for release. I slip a finger inside of her, feeling her wetness and warmth. I start to move my finger in and out, curling it up to hit her g-spot.

She moans louder, her body shaking as she reaches her climax. I can feel her pussy clenching around my finger, and I know that she's coming hard. I continue to lick and tease her as she rides out her orgasm, her body trembling with pleasure.

As she comes down from her high, she collapses on top of me, her body spent. I hold her close, feeling her heart beating against mine. We lay there for a few moments, our bodies tangled together, but as the silence grows, I can feel the tension building between us once again.

Bella looks up at me, her eyes filled with longing. "I want to make you feel good," she says, her voice low and sultry.

I smile, my heart fluttering with excitement. "I'm all yours," I say, my voice barely above a whisper.

Bella's eyes light up, and she starts to kiss my neck, her lips leaving a trail of fire along my skin. I can feel her hands roaming my body, touching and caressing my curves. I moan as she moves lower, her lips tracing patterns along my inner thigh.

"Do you have any toys?" she asks, her voice filled with curiosity.

I pause, my mind flashing back to the knife Jessica had gifted me once. But I quickly shake the thought away, not wanting to ruin the mood with it for now, we can bring her out at the farmhouse. "No, I don't," I say, my voice low and husky.

Bella nods, her hands continuing to explore my body. She slips a finger inside of me, and I moan with pleasure. She starts to move her finger in and out, her pace quickening as I grow wetter.

"Yes, just like that baby!" I gasp, my hips grinding against her hand.

Bella continues to pleasure me, her fingers moving in and out of me with ease. I can feel myself growing closer and closer to the edge, my body trembling with pleasure.

"Come for me, Baby," Bella whispers, her breath hot against my skin.

And with that, I let go, my orgasm washing over me in waves of pleasure. I can feel my body trembling, and I can hear Bella's soft moans of satisfaction, I have needed this, her, for a while and I can't wait to see how long I can keep this going for before she meets her brutal end, my last baby girl.

As we both get ourselves redressed once again, Bella and I both smile at each other, like school children or at least two lesbians who've had their first fuck. I look at her, my eyes filled with warmth.

"Bella, do you still want to come to the farmhouse with me?" I ask, hoping that she'll say yes.

Bella nods, her eyes shining. "Yes, but I need to go see my mum first. Do you want to come with me?"

I hesitate for a moment, but then I nod. "Of course, I do," I say, knowing that I want to be there for Bella, no matter what.

As we get dressed, I can't help but feel a sense of excitement. I know that these moments with Bella are precious, and I don't want to waste a single one.

As we're about to leave, I remember something. "Hey Bella, do you want me to add you to my notebook?" I ask, holding up my trusty journal.

Bella looks at me, her eyes sparkling with curiosity. "Will you fuck me in it?" she asks, a mischievous grin spreading across her face.

I laugh, my heart swelling with love for her. "Maybe, we'll see," I say, leaning in to kiss her gently on the lips.

Bella wraps her arms around me, pulling me close. "I want to get to know you more," I say, my lips brushing against hers.

Bella smiles, her eyes shining with happiness. "Me too," she says, kissing me back.

As we pull away, I can't help but remember her tattoo. "Hey, what's that dolphin all about?" I ask, trying to hide my amusement.

Bella looks down, blushing. "Oh, that's just my dolphin riding a dick tattoo," she says, a wicked grin spreading across her face.

I laugh, my heart swelling with love for her. "You fucking lunatic Bella," I say, shaking my head in disbelief.

Bella grins and takes my hand, and together we head out the door.

Bella and I make our way out of her apartment and towards her car. She leads me to a sleek black BMW, and I can't help but feel a twinge of fear. I've only known Bella for a small while and now I'm meeting her family. It all feels so personal, so real.

As we drive to the hospital, I can't help but notice how much Bella reminds me of all the other girls I've been with, aside from the fiery red hair. She's confident, strong, and independent - everything I've always been attracted to. But I know that I can't continue this life, seducing and then killing these women. "I need to change, I need to be caught," I think to myself.

Bella glances over at me, a small smile on her lips. "Is everything okay?" she asks, concern etched on her face.

I nod, forcing a smile. "Yeah, everything's fine," I say, trying to push the thoughts out of my mind.

But as we pull up to the hospital, I can't help but wonder if I can still fuck in prison, selfish but true. I've seen

"Orange is the New Black," and it seems like it could be a possibility. I push the thought out of my mind as we make our way into the hospital to see Bella's mother.

As we walk down the hospital hallway, I can't help but feel a sense of unease. I know that I can't continue this cycle of seduction and murder, but I can't imagine a life without the thrill. I wonder if I'll ever be able to change in there. But for now, I push the thoughts away, focusing on being there for Bella in this moment, just for this moment. I must gain her trust enough to bring her back to the farmhouse.

When we enter the ward room, I see a woman lying in the bed, her face pale and drawn. Bella rushes to her side, taking her hand in hers.

"Mum, this is my friend, Dahlia," Bella says, introducing me.

I step forward, offering a small wave. "Nice to meet you, Mrs. Swan," I say, trying to keep my voice steady.

Mrs. Swan turns her head towards me, her eyes focusing with effort. "Hello, dear. Bella has told me so much about you, please call me Clarice!" she says, her voice hoarse.

I force a smile, unsure of what to say. I've never been good with situations like this, especially when I'm planning on killing the person's daughter.

Clarice's appearance is a stark reminder of Bella's own mortality, and it sends a shiver down my spine. Her hair is the same fiery red as Bella's, but it's streaked with grey and thinning. Her skin is pale and papery, and her body is frail and withered. I can see the resemblance between the two of them, and it makes me feel even guiltier for what I have planned somewhat.

I take a deep breath, trying to push the thoughts out of my head. I need to focus on the present, on being here for Bella, even if it's all just a facade.

"Hey she barely knows me but we've been acquainted" I say, forcing a smile. "I'm glad that Bella has you in her life."

Clarice smiles back, her eyes glinting with warmth. "And I'm glad to have her. She's the light of my life."

Bella turns to me, her eyes shining with gratitude. "Thank you for coming, Dahlia," she says, her voice low.

I nod, my heart swelling with mild guilt.

FOURTEEN

It had been several years since I last let myself indulge in the thrill of the hunt, but I can feel the urge building inside of me once again. Joey's death still lingers in my mind every single day, a constant reminder of the power I hold over life and death. And now, I can't help but feel like finding another woman to kill is the ultimate revenge to Larissa, who had betrayed me all those years ago.

The air was thick with the scent of stale alcohol and the faint hum of desperation that lingered in the dimly lit bar. Neon lights flickered, casting an eerie glow over the crowd, illuminating the faces of those who sought solace in the shadows. The sticky floors and smoky atmosphere created a tableau of urban decay, where every corner whispered tales of lost hope and broken lives.

Amidst the chaos, I moved with the precision of a predator. My eyes, cold and calculating, scanned the room with a predatory intensity, searching for the next flicker of life to extinguish. Joey's death still haunted me, a spectre that reminded me of the power I wielded over life and death. But this was different. This was personal. Larissa's betrayal had been a wound that festered, and now, with each kill, I felt a twisted sense of vengeance.

My gaze locked onto a blonde woman, her laughter echoing through the room like a symphony of vulnerability. Hannah. Her drunken smile was intoxicating, a facade that hid the fragility beneath. She stumbled slightly, her movements uncertain, as if the weight of the world was too much to bear. I approached her, my movements deliberate, my intentions clear. When I bought her a drink, it was not an act of kindness but a strategic move, a step in a dance of death.

As we talked, her confidence began to wane, replaced by a growing sense of trust that I nurtured with calculated ease. When I asked her to come back to my place, she hesitated, her eyes reflecting a mix of curiosity and fear. But she agreed, her voice barely audible, a whisper of acquiescence that sent a chill down my spine.

The taxi ride back was a blur of anticipation, the night air rushing past us as we drove under the cover of darkness. The car's interior was filled with a tense silence, the air thick with unspoken words and ominous.

When we arrived, I helped her undress, my hands trembling with a mix of excitement and anticipation. The bedroom was consumed by a passionate embrace, our bodies intertwining as the line between desire and destruction blurred.

As I lay her on the bed, the weight of her body against mine was both exhilarating and suffocating. I went down on her, my tongue exploring her with a hunger that was both sensual and brutal. The sounds of her pleasure filled the room, a symphony of surrender that fuelled my desire. But this was more than just passion; it was a hunt, a chase that ended in the ultimate conquest.

In a seamless transition just like I had mastered before, my demeanour shifted from seduction to murder. The knife, a cold and efficient tool, glided through her flesh with a precision that was almost ritualistic. The power of life and death rested in my hands, a responsibility I embraced with a twisted sense of pride. The sight of blood, the feel of the knife, the sounds of her last breath—all sensory details that heightened the darkness of the scene.

After the murder, I meticulously disposed of the body, chopping it into pieces and stuffing it into a suitcase. My methodicalness was a testament to my control, each action deliberate and calculated. As I worked, I reflected on my satisfaction, the temporary relief I felt after each kill, a fleeting sense of power that propelled me forward.

The next morning, I made my way to the farm, my mind already planning the next hunt. The pigs would feast on Hannah's remains, a grotesque cycle of life and death that mirrored my own existence. But the thrill was fading, this kills becoming more sloppy, more boring. A clear sign of my growing addiction to the power it provided.

As I left the farm, the cool night air hitting my face, I felt alive, invigorated, and ready for another hunt.

The thrill of the chase once again, the power of life and death, was an addiction I could not resist. Each kill provided a fleeting sense of control, a temporary escape from the chaos of my own mind. But deep down, I knew the consequences were inevitable, a reckoning that loomed on the horizon.

In the darkness of my soul, I embraced the crimson obsession, a testament to my own descent into madness. Each kill was a step further into the abyss, a journey without return, where the line between predator and prey blurred into oblivion.

As I drove away from the farm, the cool night air hitting my face, I couldn't help but chuckle to myself. Who knew that being a cold-blooded killer could come with such a side of dark humour? I mean, here I was, a modern-day femme fatale, playing the role of a butcher while the pigs feasted on my leftovers. I could practically hear them squealing their appreciation for my culinary skills. "Bon appétit, my porcine friends!" I thought, wondering if they'd be able to tell the difference between gourmet and fast food. Perhaps I should start a new trend: "Farm-to-table, but make it sinister." I laughed softly at the absurdity of it all, revelling in the thrill of the hunt while contemplating how I could turn my rather peculiar hobby into a quirky cooking show. "Welcome to 'Chop It Like It's Hot'—where we serve up the freshest cuts of life!" I mused, the irony of my situation only adding to the exhilaration of my dark escapade.

As I sat behind the wheel of my car, the steering wheel felt like an extension of my hands, guiding me through the labyrinth of life. The act of driving had become more than just a skill; it was a metaphor for my journey. Each turn of the wheel, each shift of the gear, was a step towards a future filled with uncertainties and potential dangers. The road ahead was a mirror of my internal struggles, reflecting the chaos and confusion that often consumed me.

Completing my driving lessons was a pivotal moment in my life. It represented a newfound sense of control and independence, a freedom I had long craved. The challenges I faced during those lessons—navigating busy streets, mastering parallel parking, and staying calm in high-pressure situations—were not just about learning to drive but about finding strength within myself. Each obstacle overcome was a testament to my resilience, a reminder that I could rise above the circumstances that often held me back.

The car I had gone for was a sleek and modern Audi, was a reflection of my desire for nice things. Its polished exterior, a shade of deep indigo, it looked beautiful in the sun.

Yet, amidst this sense of accomplishment, I found myself drawn to darker corners of my existence. The pressures of life, combined with the weight of my past, became too much to bear. I turned to pornography and drugs as a means of escape, seeking solace in the temporary oblivion they provided. These habits became a crutch, a way to numb the pain and silence the voices that whispered of my failures and fears.

The nights were especially lonely, consumed by the glow of my computer screen and the haze of substances that clouded my mind. Pornography offered a fleeting escape, a fantasy world where I could lose myself in the illusion of connection and desire. Drugs, on the other hand, numbed the emotional pain, creating a cocoon of detachment where I could temporarily forget the struggles that defined my life.

But even in this darkness, the thoughts of my next kill lingered, a haunting reminder of the violence that had become a part of me. These thoughts were like shadows, ever-present and inescapable, shaping my decisions and influencing my actions. The line between reality and fantasy blurred, and I found myself caught in a cycle of addiction and violence, unable to break free.

As I drove through the night, the neon lights of the kebab shops of the city reflecting in my windshield, I couldn't help but wonder if I would ever find the strength to break free from this cycle. The road ahead was filled with potential dangers, both external and internal, and I knew that the choices I made would determine the course of my life.

In the quiet sanctuary of my notebooks, I find solace in the meticulous art of refining and enhancing its contents. Each page, once a mix match of rubbish, now teems with life, transformed by my pen into a world of descriptive deaths and electrifying sex scenes. It's a dark, intense narrative that mirrors the chaos of my thoughts. Yet, amidst this turmoil, I stumble upon the peculiar challenge of drawing—particularly the eyes.

My attempts at capturing the human form are often clumsy, and my sketches of eyes, though intended to be the soul's window, frequently resemble something more akin to abstract art. There's a humorous absurdity in my quest for perfection, as if each misplaced line or overly expressive pupil is a testament to my artistic aspirations.

Yet, amidst these comic failures, there's one thing I've mastered: Jessica's knife.

This knife, with its striking red handle, is not just a weapon in my narrative; it's a symbol. The red handle, vibrant and bold, demands attention, much like Jessica herself. It's a detail I've obsessed over, not just for its visual impact but for the story it tells—a story of passion, violence, and connection.

Drawing this knife is an act of precision, a moment where my artistic struggles dissolve into clarity. The red handle, glistening with an almost otherworldly intensity, is a constant reminder of Jessica's influence on my life. It's a humorous paradox—this violent object, so meticulously rendered, symbolising both destruction and creation.

In a way, the knife's red handle is a beacon of my creative journey. It stands out, vibrant and unapologetic, much like the humour I've injected into my storytelling. It's a reminder that even in the darkest of narratives, there's room for levity, for finding the absurdity in our pursuits and the humour in our imperfections.

So, as I continue to tweak and refine my notebooks, I do so with a smile, knowing that each flawed sketch and each meticulously drawn knife is part of a larger, more complex story—one that's as much about humour and humanity as it is about darkness and desire. I hope one day I'm discovered, but I have one kill in me left.

Mrs. Swan

FIFTEEN

Mrs. Swan was a figure that seemed to embody both fragility and resilience, a delicate balance that was as striking as it was poignant. Thin and wiry, her frame seemed almost delicate, as if a gust of wind could carry her away. Her hair, a fiery red that once probably commanded attention, was now interspersed with strands of grey, giving her an air of faded vibrancy. It framed her face in a wild halo, contrasting sharply against her pallor, which spoke of countless hours spent indoors, perhaps lost in thought or memories of better days.

Her withered look, a combination of age and weariness, told stories of a life lived with both joy and sorrow. Deep lines etched across her forehead hinted at the burdens she carried, while her eyes, though clouded, still sparkled with a flicker of warmth and wisdom. It was easy to see how Bella had inherited that same fiery spirit, tempered by her mother's experiences.

On several days, Bella had insisted I accompany her on a stroll to visit her mother in hospital . I recalled the way she tugged at my arm with an urgency that was both endearing and relentless. The thought of the farmhouse—the creaking floors, the dusty corners, the lingering scent of old wood— had been pushed to the back of my mind, overshadowed by the anticipation of seeing Mrs. Swan, who always had a way of drawing you in with her stories and warmth.

As we walked, Bella chatted animatedly, her voice a juxtaposition to the sombreness of her mother's appearance. I could sense a mixture of excitement and trepidation in her demeanour. The farmhouse, with its peeling paint and sprawling fields, was a mere backdrop to the emotional landscape we were about to enter.

Approaching her old house, I could already see Mrs. Swan standing at the door, her figure a silhouette against the light streaming from within. Despite her withered appearance, there was a vitality in the way she moved, a testament to her enduring spirit. Bella's mother greeted us with a smile that warmed the chilly air.

Mrs. Swan—Clarice, as she insisted I call her—had left the hospital a few weeks after her stroke, her diagnosis a stark reminder of how life can shift in an instant. The stroke had left her left side partially disabled, a fact that was both heartbreaking and oddly endearing. She moved with a determined limp, her once-slender frame now slightly askew, as if she were a character in a badly choreographed dance. Her red hair, though streaked with strands of grey, still retained its fiery intensity, framing her face like a halo of defiance. Despite her withered appearance, there was a quiet strength in her presence, a refusal to let her circumstances define her.

Clarice had always been a force to be reckoned with Bella had told me, even before the stroke. She had a way of making you feel both insignificant and important at the same time, as if she saw right through you and yet still found you worth the effort. Her house, with its peeling paint and overgrown garden, was as much a part of her as the stories she told. But now, the thought of visiting her had taken precedence over everything else, pushing the farmhouse itself into the shadows of my mind.

In between my shifts at the coffee shop, I found myself juggling the demands of my job with the less-than-noble pursuits of my personal life. There was the porn addiction, a guilty pleasure that I indulged in when the world felt too overwhelming, and the occasional smoke of cannabis, which I only indulged in when Bella wasn't around. It wasn't exactly the life I had envisioned for myself, but it was the life I had, and Clarice's resilience had a way of making me feel like I could handle it all.

Visiting her was always a mix of dread and comfort. Dread because I knew she could see right through me, and comfort because she still made me feel like I was worth her time. As I walked to her house, the knife with its bright red handle always seemed to weigh a little heavier in my pocket, as if it were a symbol of the chaos I was trying to keep at bay. Clarice may have been withered, but she was still a force to be reckoned with.

Clarice sat in her chair, her frail frame slightly hunched, yet her eyes remained sharp and piercing. I approached cautiously, feeling a mix of guilt and anxiety. Bella, standing by the window, fidgeted nervously, her presence a testament to the tension in the air.

Clarice's voice, slightly slurred from her stroke, broke the silence. "C-come closer," she said, her tone firm yet gentle. I hesitated for a moment before stepping forward, my heart pounding in my chest.

As I drew near, Clarice's gaze locked onto mine, her eyes searching for answers. "What plans do you have for my daughter?" she asked, her words slow but deliberate. I swallowed hard, my mind racing to find the right words.

"We care for each other," I began, my voice steady yet tinged with emotion. "I want to support Bella, to be there for her through everything."

Clarice nodded slightly, her expression softening. "I know you care," she replied, her voice barely above a whisper. "But she has changed since knowing you. She talks a lot about death and destruction, watches those horror movies with you."

I shifted uncomfortably, the weight of Clarice's words settling heavily on my shoulders. "We just... enjoy the thrill of it, you know? It's just movies, it's not real," I offered, trying to reassure her.

"Movies or not," Clarice interjected, her voice gaining a bit more strength, "it's the way she talks about it that worries me. Death, destruction... it's like she finds comfort in it."

Bella shifted from her spot by the window, her eyes darting between her mother and me. "Mum, it's just a phase. We're just having fun," she said, her voice a mix of defensiveness and uncertainty. "I promise I'm okay."

"Fun?" Clarice echoed, her voice laced with concern. "And what about the things you've told me... the things you and—" she hesitated, her eyes narrowing slightly as she pressed on, "—the things you and this one have gotten up to?"

I felt my cheeks flush, caught off guard. "We talk about it, but it's not—"

"No," Clarice interrupted, her voice rising slightly in disbelief, "you don't understand. I thought my daughter was straight! I thought I knew her."

Bella's face fell, a mix of embarrassment and frustration washing over her. "Mum, I'm still me! Just because I'm exploring doesn't mean I'm lost! You taught me to be open-minded!"

Clarice's brow furrowed, and for a moment, the room was silent, the air thick with tension. I could see the struggle in Clarice's eyes, the clash of old beliefs and the new reality. "I just… I worry. It's not just about you, Bella. It's about the choices you make—"

"For fuck sake Mum, I'm not a child anymore!" Bella shot back, her voice rising, a brave defiance in her tone. "I can handle myself. I love you, but you have to trust me!"

Clarice's gaze softened momentarily, but the concern still lingered. "I just want to know you're not dragging her into something she can't handle. I've seen her change, and I want her to be safe."

I nodded, understanding the depth of Clarice's fears. "I get that. Bella has changed, but I believe it's for the better. She's exploring who she is, and that's important."

As the conversation unfolded, the tension began to ebb, replaced by a fragile understanding. Clarice's eyes, still sharp, now held a flicker of acceptance. "I just want her to be happy," she murmured, her voice barely above a whisper.

Bella stepped forward, reaching for her mother's hand. "I am happy, Mum. I promise."

In that moment, I realised that this was more than just a conversation about relationships; it was about family, understanding, and the evolution of love in all its forms. The knife, with its bright red handle, felt like a distant memory, overshadowed by the raw emotions that filled the room. It was a moment of vulnerability, a reminder that even in the face of fear and uncertainty, love could still flourish.

As the conversation with Clarice and Bella wound down, I found myself stepping outside the house, the cool evening air wrapping around me like a comforting blanket, I wish I had some weed on my right now, but I can't, not around Bella. The stars twinkled above, their light a stark contrast to the heavy emotions swirling inside me. Clarice's words had struck a chord, and I couldn't help but let my thoughts drift to my own family, people I hadn't thought about in years.

I missed my mother and father, their faces a blur in my memory now. My mother's soft smile at the times she was happy and my father's booming laugh, the way he could make any problem seem manageable with just a few words. I hadn't gone to visit their graves in years. I felt a pang of longing, a yearning to reconnect, to bridge the gap I had created.

And then there was Ren, my older brother. We had always been close, a bond forged through countless childhood adventures and shared secrets. But life had pulled us in different directions, and now he was set to move to Scotland with Amy, his roommate. I had only met Amy once, during that particularly stressful time when I was dealing with some police situations that we don't mention any longer. She had been there for Ren, offering support and understanding when he needed it most. I couldn't help but feel a twinge of jealousy, a fear that Ren might find a new life so far away, leaving me behind.

As I stood there, the weight of my thoughts pressing down on me, I realised how much I had taken my family for granted. Clarice's concern for Bella had awakened something within me, a desire to reconnect, to build bridges before it was too late. Maybe it was time to reach out, to let Ren knew that I missed them, that I hadn't forgotten the love and support he had always offered, even when I pushed him away.

The night air grew colder, and I wrapped my arms around myself, trying to hold onto the warmth of the memories that had been stirred to life. Clarice had made me miss my mother and father, to yearn for the connection I had lost.

The knife in my pocket felt heavier with every step away from the Swan household. It pressed against my thigh, a cold, insistent reminder of the thing I had been carrying with me for weeks now. The weight of it was comforting in a way I didn't want to admit. Comforting and necessary. My fingers twitched, itching to curl around the handle, to feel the sharp edge of the blade against my skin. But I kept my hand at my side, clenched into a fist. Not yet. Not here.

The night was quiet, the kind of stillness that made the inside of my head feel louder. My thoughts raced, colliding and tangling like a storm I couldn't escape. Bella's face kept flashing in my mind—her wide, trusting eyes, the way her lips curved when she smiled, the sound of her laugh, light and carefree. It made my chest ache and twist in ways I didn't understand. I hated it. I hated her.

No. That wasn't quite right. I didn't hate her. I didn't think I could. That was the problem.

The streets were empty, the houses dark. Everyone was asleep, tucked away in their safe little lives, blissfully unaware of the kind of thoughts that could fester in someone's head. The kind of thoughts that haunted me. The kind of thoughts that made me want to press the tip of that knife into flesh, to watch the life drain out of someone who didn't deserve it—but who also did. Because Bella Swan wasn't innocent. Not really. She was a catalyst, a spark that had lit a fire inside me I didn't know how to put out.

I stopped walking, my breath coming out in short, uneven puffs that clouded in the cold air. My hand slid into my pocket, fingers brushing against the knife's handle. Just a touch, I told myself. Just to remind me it's still there. But the moment my skin made contact with the cool metal, I felt a shudder ripple through me. My heart pounded, my temples throbbed, and my thoughts spiralled.

What if I did it? Right now. What if I turned around, went back to her house, and finished what I started?

The idea was intoxicating. My pulse quickened, my body tightening with a mix of dread and anticipation. I could see it so clearly—the way her eyes would widen in surprise, the way her mouth would open, not to laugh or smile, but to scream. I could almost hear it, the sound cutting through the silence of the night. I could almost feel it, the way the knife would sink into her skin, the way her blood would stain my hands, warm and sticky.

I swallowed hard, my throat dry. My stomach churned, a sick, twisting feeling that made me want to double over. But I didn't. I stood there, gripping the knife in my pocket, my mind racing.

Bella didn't deserve it. That's what everyone would say. She was kind, smart, good. Too good for someone like me. But that was the thing—she didn't even see it. She didn't see the darkness in me, the way it clawed at the edges of my soul, threatening to consume me. She looked at me like I was something worth saving, like I was capable of being more than the sum of my broken parts. And that was the most infuriating thing of all. Because she was wrong.

I wasn't worth saving. I never had been. And maybe that was why I wanted to hurt her. Maybe I wanted to prove her wrong, to show her exactly what kind of person I was. Or maybe I just wanted to feel something, anything, even if it was pain. Even if it was hers.

I pulled the knife out of my pocket, the blade glinting in the pale moonlight. I stared at it, my reflection distorted in the polished steel. I didn't recognise the person looking back at me. Her eyes were hollow, her mouth set in a grim line. She looked like a stranger, someone capable of things I didn't want to admit. But she was there, staring back at me, daring me to make a choice.

"Do it," she whispered, her voice echoing in my head. "You know you want to."

I tightened my grip on the knife, my knuckles turning white. My heart was racing, my breath coming in shallow gasps. I could feel the urge building inside me, a slow, creeping pressure that threatened to explode. But before I could move, before I could take a single step back toward Bella's house, a sound broke through the silence.

"Hey."

I froze, my whole body going rigid. The voice was soft, hesitant, but it cut through the fog in my mind like a knife. I turned slowly, my heart pounding in my chest.

Bella stood a few feet away, her arms wrapped around herself, her eyes wide and cautious. She looked small in the dim light, her hair falling in loose waves around her face. For a moment, I just stared at her, my hand still gripping the knife at my side.

"What are you doing out here?" she asked, her voice trembling slightly.

I didn't answer. I couldn't. My mind was blank, my thoughts swirling in a chaotic mess. I wanted to tell her to leave, to run, to get as far away from me as possible. But I also wanted to pull her close, to feel the warmth of her skin against mine, to bury my face in her hair and breathe her in.

"I… I saw you leave," she said, taking a tentative step toward me. "I just… I wanted to make sure you were okay."

Her words hit me like a punch to the gut. She was worried about me. Even after everything, after the way I'd pushed her away, after the way I'd looked at her with eyes full of venom, she still cared. It made me want to scream.

"I'm fine," I said, my voice rough and strained.

She shook her head, her eyes searching mine. "You're not fine. I can see it in your face. Something's wrong. Talk to me."

I let out a bitter laugh, the sound harsh in the quiet night. "You don't want to know what's wrong, Bella. Trust me."

"I do," she said, her voice firm now. She took another step toward me, her hand reaching out like she wanted to touch me. But she stopped herself, her fingers curling into a fist. "I want to help you. Whatever it is, we can figure it out together."

I looked at her, my chest tight, my throat burning. The knife in my hand felt like it weighed a thousand pounds. I wanted to drop it, to let it fall to the ground and walk away. But I couldn't. My fingers wouldn't uncurl. My hand wouldn't move.

"You can't help me," I said, my voice barely above a whisper. "No one can."

She shook her head again, her eyes filling with tears. "That's not true. I'm here, aren't I? I'm not going anywhere."

Her words were like a knife to my heart, sharper than any blade. I wanted to believe her. I wanted to let her in, to let her see the broken, twisted mess inside me and still believe she could fix it. But I couldn't. I didn't deserve that. And she didn't deserve me.

I tightened my grip on the knife, my jaw clenching. "You should go, Bella. Now."

She didn't move. She just stood there, staring at me with those damn eyes, so full of trust and hope. It made me want to scream, to lash out, to do something, anything, to make her see the truth.

So I did.

I lunged at her, the knife flashing in the moonlight. She stumbled back, her eyes widening in shock, but she didn't run. She didn't scream. She just stood there, frozen, as I closed the distance between us.

And then I stopped. My hand trembled, the knife hovering inches from her chest. My breath came in ragged gasps, my whole body shaking.

"Run," I growled, my voice low and desperate. "Run."

She didn't. Instead, she reached out, her fingers brushing against mine. The knife fell from my hand, clattering to the ground. Her eyes never left mine, her gaze steady and unafraid.

"I'm not going anywhere," she said softly. "Not without you."

I stared at her, my chest heaving, my mind spinning. And then, without thinking, I grabbed her, pulling her into me. My lips crashed against hers, hard and desperate. She gasped into the kiss, her hands clutching at my shoulders, her body pressing against mine. It was messy, frenzied, wrong. But it was also the only thing that felt right.

I kissed her like I wanted to destroy her, like I wanted to erase every trace of her from the world. But she kissed me back like I was something worth saving, like I was more than the sum of my broken parts. And for a moment, just a moment, I almost believed her.

But then the knife was there, lying on the ground between us, a stark reminder of who I really was. And in that moment, I knew I had to choose.

To destroy her or to let her destroy me.

I pulled away, my breath ragged, my heart pounding. Bella looked up at me, her lips swollen, her eyes wide and searching.

"What are you doing?" she whispered.

I stepped back, my hands shaking, my mind racing. The knife was still there, lying on the ground, taunting me.

"I don't know," I said, my voice breaking. "I don't know."

She reached for me, her hand trembling as it brushed against mine. "Let me help you," she said softly. "Please."

I looked at her, my chest tight, my throat burning. And then, without another word, I turned and walked away, leaving her standing there in the cold, dark night. The knife was still on the ground, but it wasn't gone. It would never be gone.

And neither would she.

I walked away from Bella, my heart pounding, but her voice cut through the chaos in my mind: "Wait!"

I froze, every instinct screaming for me to keep moving. I turned slowly. Fear twisted in my gut as I saw her sprinting toward me, the determination in her eyes a mirror to the storm inside my head.

"I... I picked up your notebook," she panted, holding it out like it was a lifeline. My chest tightened.

"You shouldn't have read that," I snapped, the anger boiling over. The things I wrote were the darkest corners of my mind, thoughts I'd never meant to expose.

"But it matters," Bella said, her voice steady, unwavering against my rage. "You don't have to hide from me. I read what you wrote about Jessica, and it's not just a weird fantasy. It's real, and I want to help you understand it."

Her words cut deeper than any blade. Jessica wasn't some trivial crush; she was a reflection of my own twisted despair, a target for my rage—a rage I could unleash. I had poured my heart and my darkness into those pages, and here was Bella, trying to peel back the layers, trying to see the monster underneath.

"You shouldn't have seen that!" I spat, clenching my fists. "You're delusional if you think there's anything I can talk about that won't hurt you."

"Maybe I don't care about that," she shot back, stepping closer, unfazed by my aggression. "You think you're a monster, but I see you. I see the parts of you that are scared, that are hurting. I want to understand you, even if it's ugly."

The sincerity in her expression made my heart ache, but it also sent a fresh wave of anger coursing through me. I looked down, my mind racing. I wanted to scream, to unleash the darkness that clawed at me, but a part of me yearned for her to see the truth—the truth that I was a potential threat, a danger to anyone who dared to get too close.

"You're so damn persistent," I said, fighting to rein in my spiralling thoughts. "Why can't you see that I'm dangerous? That I could hurt you? I don't want to drag you down with me."

"Maybe I don't care about that," she responded, her voice firm. "I'm here, right now. I want to know who you really are, the parts you think you can hide."

A fire ignited in her eyes, drawing me in. It was a challenge, a dare. But in that moment, I felt a descent into darkness pulling me back down. As much as I wanted to connect with her, I could still picture the knife in my hand, the way it glinted under the moonlight, the intoxicating idea of taking her life—a life that didn't deserve to end but felt like it would give me some kind of twisted release.

"Okay," I whispered, and the admission tasted bitter on my tongue. "But you have to promise me—if it gets too dark, you'll run. You can't save me. I'm a mess."

"I'm not going anywhere," she replied, steel in her voice. "I'm here for you. Always."

I felt the tremor of conflicting emotions tighten around my chest. As I stared at her, I could see the light in her eyes but also the fragility of it. What if I extinguished that light? The thought sent a shudder down my spine.

"Then get ready for the truth," I said, each word heavy with what I was concealing. "You think you want to understand me. You have no idea what that could cost you."

I tried to step back, to regain control over my thoughts, but a cold rage bubbled to the surface. I could feel the darkness beckoning, whispering promises of relief and chaos. What if I turned that knife on Bella?

Suddenly, I lunged forward, that small voice urging me to reach my breaking point. "You want the truth?" I growled, looking deep into her eyes, searching for a flicker of fear, but finding only defiance.

But before I could stop myself, I caught her wrist, holding her in place. "You really don't get it, do you? I could hurt you. I could end you. And it—god, it might feel good. It might be the only way I can finally let go of this hell inside of me."

She gasped, and I could see the weight of my words hit her. In that instant, I saw the fear flash across her face, but she didn't pull away. She stood her ground, keeping her gaze steady on me, filled with a reckless courage that made my insides churn.

"Run, Bella. Please." I pleaded, my voice cracking as I fought the urge to hurt her. "I don't think I can control myself."

But something snapped.

Maybe it was the despair, the overwhelming sense that I was beyond salvation, or maybe it was the bloodlust that had settled deep in my bones. I clenched my teeth, wrestling with the urge. My pulse raced with terrifying exhilaration, like I was teetering at the edge of a precipice.

She stepped forward, and I felt my resolve start to fray further. I could feel the darkness wrapping its claws around my heart, threatening to break free.

"I'm not going anywhere," she said softly, resolute. "You have to face this."

With that, the tension snapped, and in a moment of pure instinct, I found myself pushing her back, heart racing as the knife of my thoughts pierced through the haze of reality. The predator and the prey. Would I be the one that walked away, or would we both succumb to the chaos within?

Everything hung in the balance—a precipice that promised either freedom or damnation—for both of us. The knife could either sever the last thread of hope or finally cut through the darkness.

And before I could decide, I lunged forward, the world locked in a violent stillness as I teetered on the edge of my fate.

At The Crossroads

SIXTEEN

The moment I lunged, everything slowed: the air settled thick around us, panic skimming the surface of my skin. But instead of the knife sinking into flesh, I stumbled back, my mind throwing up walls between my desperate intentions and the very real, warm presence of Bella before me.

"I don't know what the fuck to do!" I shouted, the words erupting from my throat like a dam breaking. I turned and took off, running faster than I ever had in my life, fuelled by a cocktail of fear, rage, and the chilling clarity that I could not be trusted.

I could hear her footsteps behind me, pounding against the pavement like a relentless drumbeat, but I didn't dare look back. Every muscle in my body screamed for me to keep moving, to escape the chaos of my mind and the warmth of her presence that had confused me for too long.

"Dahlia, wait!" Bella called after me, her voice both breathless and determined. A part of me hated that she was chasing me, determined to keep this twisted connection alive, but the other part—well, that part thrived on the adrenaline and the chaos.

As I sprinted towards the farmhouse, my mind churned with memories I couldn't reconcile. Those moments flashed before me—her first visit to my café, the way she lit up the room with her laughter, the conversations we'd shared that felt like threads pulling us closer together. And then, that day in the park, sitting under the sun with her head resting on my shoulder, the kiss we'd shared that sent jolts of heat through my entire body. Beautiful memories paired with blood-soaked fantasies of violence.

Why was my brain fucking up now? Why was it so hard to untangle the goodness of her smile from the darkness festering inside me? I slammed to a stop outside the farmhouse, hands on my knees, panting hard, and finally dared to look back.

Bella caught up beside me, breathing just as heavily. Her expression was a mix of concern and amusement, which only made my heart race faster. "You're, like, really fast," she huffed, a teasing tone slipping through her breathlessness as she leaned against the railing. "You should consider track or something."

I let out a shaky laugh, the absurdity of the situation hitting me. Here we were, my heart still roaring from nearly losing control, and yet there was Bella, trying to lighten the tension after I'd just nearly admitted to wanting to kill her.

"Yeah, right. Who needs a track when I could just run from my problems?" I replied, wiping sweat from my forehead with a shaky hand.

She shifted closer, eyes locking onto mine. "Dahlia, I don't care what you are or what you think you're capable of. You're not fucking killing me. At least not without fucking me first."

Her words caught me off guard, and for the briefest moment, arousal cut through the adrenaline. Fire flickered in her gaze, daring me to confront the truth I was desperately trying to avoid. That desperation and twisted need had become interwoven with my perception of her.

My chest heaved as I wrestled with the weight of both desire and hatred. I thought back to the intimacy we had shared, the way our bodies moved together, heat and urgency blending into something almost perfect. But just as quickly, the clearer the memory came, the louder the demons grew in my mind, wrestling for dominance.

"Bella, I–" I started, but my voice trailed off, the fog of confusion thickening.

"Dahlia," she said, cutting through my spiralling thoughts, her voice steady. "You can fight this. Whatever this is, I won't let you push me away. You don't have to face it alone."

The sincerity in her eyes broke through my bravado, slashing through the tangled mess inside me. And yet, the knife metaphorically at my back was still whispering. What if I lost control again? What if I lashed out, letting my instincts win?

I didn't want to think about that. "You shouldn't be here," I blurted, looking away, heart racing as I turned my back on her. "You really need to run. Just… just leave me alone!"

But I could hear her footsteps echoing my own, and it felt like a noose tightening around my throat. The push and pull of wanting to protect her at all costs and the terrifying urge to let my darkness consume us both felt insurmountable.

The ground beneath me felt unsteady, each breath a battle against the unraveling tension. I didn't know where this would lead—whether I'd find the strength to break free of my murky past or whether I would drown us both in chaos.

And for the first time, I stood at a crossroads that could tear two souls apart or bind us together in our shared fear—either way, something was about to snap, and I was all too aware that my next move could change everything.

The sound of Bella's footsteps echoed like the ticking of a clock, counting down to an inevitable showdown—a moment where chaos collided with the heavy weight of desire and regret. I shifted away from her, unwilling to let the warmth of her presence distract me from the emerging threat, but even more reluctant to confront the swirling darkness inside me.

"Dahlia," she said softly, inching closer despite the tension, her voice steady and resolute. "You're stronger than this. Please don't push me away."

I turned my gaze towards the shadows of the trees, where the figure loomed. A familiar ache tugged at me, a mix of anger and longing that bled into memories of my brother, Ren. Those moments where laughter echoed through our childhood home, the warmth of his presence grounding me amid a tempest of chaos.

"Yeah, just Ren," I replied bitterly, the words slipping from my lips before I could rethink them. "He was the one who had it all figured out. I blew it all, and now look where I am." I laughed, but it was hollow, devoid of the warmth I dredged up in those rare lighter moments. "Now I'm just standing here, ready to dive into madness, while you and my brother both have it all together."

Bella's brow furrowed, and her voice held a gentle challenge, "And me. You have me too, Dahlia. I'm right here. You're not alone."

That only stoked the rage bubbling within me. "You don't get it! Ren was the strong one. He brought light to everyone he met. And then I—" I caught myself, gripping my hair in frustration. "I just destroyed everything."

I could see Bella's eyes flash with hurt, but I was too lost in my spiralling thoughts to care. All I could feel was the confusion and that ruthless urge clawing at my insides. That sickening thought that whispered maybe I should. Maybe I should unleash everything I felt suppressed, even the darker, unbearable need to take her—a violent freedom wrapped in twisted desire.

"Dahlia, I want to understand," she pushed back, steady, unfaltering. "But shoving me away isn't going to solve anything. I don't want you to be alone in this."

"Shut up!" I shouted, the words raw and invasive, cutting through the haze of my thoughts. "You think you can save me? You think you have the strength to handle this?" I stepped toward her, feeling the urgency rise as the figure remained close, measuring us with that sinister grin, but now my attention was split. "You don't realise how much worse it is. You don't really know what I'm capable of."

"Then show me," she urged, an unquenchable fire sparking in her gaze. The resolve in her voice made something inside me roar with fury and something else—something darker.

I gritted my teeth, wrestling against that bitter urge that gnawed at me. The very thought of hurting her felt like chains wrapping tighter around my core.

A flicker of light danced at the edge of my memories, the times Ren had shielded me from the world. He had always been the one to guide me, to pull me from the darkness that threatened to consume. But now, here I was, at the precipice of self-destruction, and I could feel the whispers of the past clawing at my mind. "Even Ren couldn't save me from myself."

"Dahlia, please!" Bella implored, stepping closer, her eyes softening despite the tension hanging in the air. "Fight against it. Don't let it win. Whatever you're feeling right now—"

The sense of impending violence surged in me, trying to drown everything else. I could feel the war in my very bones, that duality of wanting to protect and simultaneously destroy. It surged to the forefront. "I want to fight it, I do! But you make it worse, Bella! You make this urge to kill you so much stronger than anyone else."

At that moment, the figure in the shadows stepped closer, silhouetted against the dim light filtering through the trees. "Troubling, isn't it? That you could need her so much, yet the urge to end her is stronger than any care you think you hold."

"Shut up!" I snapped at the figure. It carried Mother's voice, mocking me with reminders of my failures, beckoning me to give in to the darkness. With each passing second, the shadows twisted and stretched around us, threatening to tear away any semblance of control I had left. Have I finally gone mad? I always powered through life with a smile, knowing I had never been depressed, anxious, bat shit crazy! Just fuelled by the adrenaline of blood.

Bella's presence felt tenuous against that rising tide of all of this, and the grip of my anger tightened harder around my throat. Gone had the days of turning the darkness I wanted to create into a life long sitcom of humour.

The battle raged in my mind—every part of me screaming to trust her, to believe she could save me while another part itched to lash out, to unleash everything I had held back. I wanted to get fucking caught this time, an infamous serial killer, a woman, a woman that got away with it for so long.

"Dahlia," Bella said, drawing closer, her gaze glowing with an intensity I both craved and feared. "You know I'm right. I can help you. You have to stop fighting."

"Not this time," I growled through gritted teeth, battling against the inherent rage suffocating all the light around us. "I'm tired of fighting. I want it to end!" I turned slightly towards her, the darkness threatening to smother me, a twisted smirk creeping back across the figure's face, mirroring my inner chaos. "And you have no idea what that means."

In that breath, I felt something break within me. The core of my being trembled with the weight of choice—between the twisted urge to embrace the violent past I fought against and the shining spectre of a future I couldn't grasp.

With a sudden, primal scream, I charged at the figure, hand outstretched, ready to sink into the abyss and drag Bella with me, my internal war clashing in a cacophony of momentary clarity and relentless chaos.

But just as I drew near, something held me back—a force anchoring me to reality. In the blink of an eye, I turned back to Bella, desperation pulsing through me, raw and aching.

Shock and fear cascaded across her features, and I could see the conflict in her eyes—the desire to understand but intertwined with the fear of the monster I could become. "Dahlia, don't—"

And then, everything erupted.

"Dahlia!" Bella screamed, but the darkness was closing in. As I lunged, caught between worlds, one thought pierced through the chaos: it was already too late.

The shadows engulfed me, and as the world faded, my final plea echoed in that suffocating void—could I fight this, or had I already lost everything, including her? One thing I knew for sure was that I had certainly lost my god damn fucking mind.

EPILOGUE

I always thought of myself as the hunter, and Dahlia? She was the prey—an unsuspecting mouse scurrying through my carefully laid traps. From the first moment I set foot in that café, I knew I was more than just a customer, more than just a girl with a craving for a cappuccino. I was there to claim her, to unravel her, to see if she could be moulded into someone worthy of my affection —or my malice.

Dahlia moved through her world with an air of distracted grace, her mind always somewhere else. I watched her work aimlessly behind the counter, her fingers dancing over the register while her thoughts seemed to drift into darker realms. There was something hypnotic about her lack of awareness, a kind of chaos that drew me in like a moth to a flame. That scrappy little cafe filled with the smell of burnt coffee beans and succulent croissant became my hunting ground, a stage where I choreographed my every move to her rhythm.

When I first read her notebooks, my heart raced with an excitement I hadn't felt in years. There it was—the delicate line she walked between creation and destruction. I sensed it immediately; she was a killer in her own right. The way she penned her thoughts—the confusion, the longing, the violent desires —it all rang true to me. But her words were sloppy and unrefined, mere hints of the darkness that lay simmering below the surface. She was pathetic in some ways, good at sex but lacking the finesse to truly control her desires.

What a clueless bitch, I thought more than once, smirking to myself as I crafted my plan to wind my way into her life. I wanted to show her what true pleasure was—the kind that crept in like frost and left one breathless. I craved the thrill of tight ropes and whispered commands, a taste of the exquisite pain married with ecstasy.

Dahlia didn't even have toys for fuck sake, such a boring bitch.. How quaint. I, on the other hand, loved to fuck, but I needed more than just bodies; I needed submission. There was beauty in domination, in drawing someone to the brink and watching them teeter over the edge.

But those pleasures? They had to take a backseat for a time. By the time she let me in, she had unwittingly accelerated my darker appetites. I started to see her— perhaps too clearly. I revelled in the thought of killing her, my vicious affection morphing into a consuming obsession. I envisioned it for weeks; the way it would feel to take everything she was and extinguish it.

I lost count of my victims, the faces and names blended into a beautiful tapestry of fear and finality. Each death was an art form, an intimate dance that I choreographed with the same precision I used to plan my entrance into Dahlia's world. I wasn't even from this godforsaken town. I was a ghost - an outsider passing through, on a vicious pilgrimage to cleanse the filth I found in my trail.

My hands tingled with memories of my first kill, a boy named Jake who had tormented me in secondary school. I had been waiting for just the right moment to , drive him into submission, and drown him in the lake—the place he thought was safe. It was poetic, a fitting end to his torment of me. I learned quickly that drowning was such a peaceful way to take a life.

Another time, I choked the life out of a girl who thought she could dance too close to my man. Crumpling her small body into the boot of my car felt all too easy; I tossed her into a field and left her to the wild. All of those dark fantasies culminated into an intoxicating high that sent ripples of adrenaline skimming through my veins. At least the idea of feeding bodies to the pigs—like Dahlia cleverly did I must say —would have brought a disturbing humour to the horror of it all. But I preferred fire; there was something timely, something cleansing about watching my prey turn to ash, leaving nothing behind but faint memories swirling in the breeze.

And then, there was Harvey Benjamin Wright, the partner in my crime. A man with the charm of a snake and the mind of a killer. He lived abroad and we shared secret emails—a grotesque exchange of tactics that unfolded like twisted blueprints for our violent designs. From strangulation to drowning, I learned the methods of killing like I was taking a masterclass in horror. We've met several times, in England and where he was in Spain, he fucked like a God.

It was not just about the thrill for him or for me; it was a dangerous game of chess, moving pieces across a board where killing was our strategy, and survival was the prize. I could almost hear his voice whispering through the lines of our correspondence, giving me the courage to carry out my desires.

What could have been just another reckless interaction instead became my obsession. I wanted Dahlia, wanted to introduce her to my world. Instead, I suddenly found myself wanting to tear her apart piece by piece. Each moment trailing her had fuelled my fury and fascination. She was the perfect storm, and I was caught in the eye.

As it turned out, my plans to woe her smoothly transitioned quite well. I watched her, waiting for the right moment. I'd invite: her to meet my family, make her think I wanted a future with her. But beneath that beautiful veneer of domesticity lay my true intentions—to drown the fucking monster she thought she was, metaphorically of course, I had killed her better than that.

What did she want? Fame? Fortune? Her notebooks just that of a naive little girl. Amateur.

Oh baby girl, I'll finish your novel for you and take it further than you ever would have. Unlike you, I don't want to get caught.

For I'm not Bella, I'm not who you think I am. I've been Margot, Julia, Kaitlin, you name it, nobody knows my real name aside from my actual mother, who is long dead, nobody knows who I really am. Oh, Mrs. Swan—sweet child, she was merely a frail old woman with dementia. I had met her daughter just months prior, fully aware that I'd need her mother's fragile state to execute my plan to eliminate Dahlia. I held both of them under duress, threatening to expose a secret I had uncovered about their fraudulent activities. It was sheerly fortuitous that Mrs. Swan suffered a stroke right at such a pivotal moment.

After our little rendezvous in that rundown farmhouse, I managed to snap Dahlia, this time using her greatest weakness—her insatiable desire for intimacy. It was no secret that she was a sucker for pleasure, and I knew just how to wet her appetite.

As I seduced her once more, a wicked smile played on my lips; I had her exactly where I wanted her. The allure of passion clouded her judgment, blinding her to the danger that lurked beneath my charming facade. Little did she know, her cravings would ultimately lead her to her demise

As the days passed, I watched Dahlia closely, biding my time. It was crucial that I strike at the perfect moment, when her guard was down. I laid the groundwork meticulously, using Mrs. Swan as a pawn to lure Dahlia into a false sense of security.

One evening, just after dusk, I invited Dahlia to Mrs. Swan's house under the pretence of wanting to surprise her with a visit. I made sure Dahlia was lulled into a relaxed state, convinced that she was simply coming to check on the old woman. I ensured that Mrs. Swan remained nonverbal and seemingly unaware, her presence merely a chilling backdrop to my intentions.

Once Dahlia arrived, I engaged her in light conversation, allowing her to reminisce about the past with Mrs. Swan. As she leaned closer to hear the frail woman's incoherent mutterings, I stealthily retrieved a small vial from my pocket. The poison within was odourless and tasteless—a perfect choice for someone as unsuspecting as Dahlia.

I pretended to lean in to whisper a secret, and with an almost casual flick of my wrist, I poured the contents of the vial into her drink. She raised the glass to her lips, oblivious to the danger lurking within.

Within moments, the effects kicked in. Dahlia's eyes widened with confusion and panic as she clutched her throat, gasping for air. It was a sight to behold—a switch from carefree to desperate, and I took great pleasure in knowing that my plan had unfolded just as I intended.

As she collapsed to the floor, I stood over her, feeling a sense of triumph wash over me. Dahlia would no longer be a threat, and with Mrs. Swan's secret safe, my own position was secure. Sometimes, it's those who are considered weak that can be the most useful in a game of life and death.

The poison I chose was 1080, commonly known as Sodium Fluoroacetate—an odourless and tasteless substance often used in pest control. It's a fast-acting agent, ensuring that Dahlia wouldn't immediately suspect foul play.

After she collapsed, I acted swiftly. I loaded her unconscious body into my car and drove her back to the farmhouse, the rural landscape shrouded in darkness. The tires crunched over gravel while I mentally prepped for the next stage of my plan.

Arriving at the farmhouse, I quickly manoeuvred her limp form into the barn, where the pigs were kept. The stench of the place was overpowering, but I welcomed it as a fitting backdrop to the grim task ahead. My heart raced with a mix of excitement and adrenaline.

I wanted to ensure that Dahlia, and any trace of her presence, vanished forever. Dragging her close to the pen, I tossed her in among the hungry swine. Their eager snouts sniffed around, the sounds of slurping and grunting filling the air as they quickly began to feast.

But it wasn't enough to rid myself of her entirely. I had to erase any evidence—every notebook, every scrap of information that could link me to her demise. I gathered her belongings, her sweet hair tangled and matted on the floor, and tossed them into a makeshift pyre I'd prepared earlier. With a flick of a match, the flames danced to life, consuming the notebooks and her hair in an inferno that crackled and hissed, sending thick black smoke billowing into the night sky.

As I watched the fire consume everything, I felt an exhilarating wave of freedom. Dahlia was gone, and with her, the weight of her past. The pigs continued to root and grumble around her, oblivious to the irony of their feast—a fitting end for someone who had meddled in affairs that were never hers to control.

Goodbye, sweet Dahlia. Your secrets have been laid bare, while mine remain securely hidden. Unlike you, I am a phantom in the shadows—one who will never taste the bitter sting of consequence.

Bella x

Printed in Great Britain
by Amazon